Sophie McKenzie

TRUTH OR DARE

SIMON &
SCHUSTER

First published in Great Britain in 2022
by Simon & Schuster UK Ltd

Text copyright © 2022 Sophie McKenzie

1 3 5 7 9 10 8 6 4 2

Simon & Schuster UK Ltd
1st Floor, 222 Gray's Inn Road, London
WC1X 8HB

www.simonandschuster.co.uk
www.simonandschuster.com.au
www.simonandschuster.co.in

Simon & Schuster Australia, Sydney
Simon & Schuster India, New Delhi

A CIP catalogue record for this book is available
from the British Library.

PB ISBN 978-1-4711-9913-4
eBook ISBN 978-1- 4711-9914-1
eAudio ISBN 978-1-4711-9929-5

Typeset in the UK by Sorrel Packham
Printed and bound by CPI Group (UK) Ltd, Croydon, CR0 4YY

MIX
Paper from
responsible sources
FSC® C171272

TRUTH
OR
DARE

**Also by
Sophie McKenzie**

Hide and Secrets
Truth or Dare

THE MISSING SERIES

Girl, Missing
Sister, Missing
Missing Me
Boy, Missing – a World Book Day £1 book

THE MEDUSA PROJECT

The Set-Up
The Hostage
The Rescue
Hunted
Double-Cross
Hit Squad

To Roger, Dana,
Alex and Charlie,
with love

ONE

The train slows to a stop somewhere between stations. On one side of the track, trees sway gently in the breeze, sunlight dancing through their bright green branches. On the other, an expanse of fields, bounded by hedges, is spread out as far as the eye can see. Each field is utterly empty: no people, no houses. Not even a cow.

This is the countryside. Where literally nothing is happening. And I'm going to be stuck here for the next six weeks.

It's my worst nightmare.

My brother Leo is sitting in the seat opposite mine. His pale, earnest face is turned, as usual, towards his phone. Leo is nine, five years younger than me, but he's not like most kids his age. He knows some things in depth, like stuff about engines and volcanoes and electricity, that your average uni professor wouldn't have a clue about. Then there's other things, like talking to people in real life, where he often acts like a tiny kid.

Mum ruffles his hair, then tucks her own behind her

1

ears. She hasn't taken her eyes off her laptop this whole journey except to dole out sandwiches for lunch an hour or so ago.

'How many more stops?' I ask, as the train starts moving again.

Mum looks up, frowning. She's always frowning these days. Mainly because she's always working. 'I'm not sure,' she says.

'I thought you grew up round here,' I persist.

The crease between her eyes deepens. 'What was the last station?' she asks.

I shrug.

'Polborne,' says Leo. I have no idea how he knows. I swear he didn't even look up when we were in the station.

Mum's eyes spark with alarm. 'Next stop then,' she says, grabbing the papers which litter our table and shoving them in her tote. 'Maya, fetch our bags, please.'

I heave a sigh and get up.

'Is that when you're leaving us, Mum?' Leo asks, a note of anxiety creeping into his voice.

'That's where Gran is picking you up,' Mum counters brightly.

I glance at Leo. His solemn eyes meet mine and I force a smile. I want to reassure him, but I'm as miserable as he is at the prospect of spending the entire summer in

Cornwall with our grandparents. Right now, back in London, my friends will be in the park – chatting and playing music and talking about the parties planned for this weekend.

And I'm missing all of it.

Leo's lower lip wobbles. I wrack my brains for something I can say to cheer him up. It's not like either of us know our grandparents that well. It's been years since we were here and we only do video calls every now and then. I fall back on something Mum mentioned last week.

'Gran and Grandad's place is near the sea,' I say. 'You'll be able to do science experiments in the rock pools or whatever.'

Leo raises his eyebrows. 'But I didn't bring my microscope,' he points out.

'I'm sure there'll be an app for that,' Mum says vaguely, now trying to ram her laptop on top of the papers in her tote. 'Maya, *please*. The bags.'

'I'm *doing* it.'

I haul Leo's bag and my suitcase down from the overhead rack. The train slows, the brakes screeching loudly as it pulls into a tiny station. Leo puts his hands over his ears; he hates loud noises.

I look out of the window. Could it be more deserted? There are weeds growing through half the cracks in the platform. I lug Leo's bag and my suitcase along the aisle. Nobody else is getting off.

'Come on, Leo,' Mum urges, her voice rising behind me. 'The noise has stopped now. Make sure you've got your phone with you, and don't forget your rucksack.'

I press the door release button and step onto the platform. After the chill of the air-conditioned carriage, the sun is fierce on my face. My suitcase is heavy, the handle digging into my palm. I set it down on the platform as Mum and Leo emerge from the train.

Leo squints up and down. 'I don't see Gran,' he says.

'She'll be out in the car park.' Mum dives into her cluttered shoulder bag and pulls out her phone. She checks the screen, an anxious expression on her face. 'Right, I've got ten minutes before my train. Mustn't miss my connection to Plymouth.'

Feeling sullen, I follow the two of them along the platform, dragging my suitcase and Leo's holdall behind me. The sun beats down on my face and back. I'm too hot in my long-sleeved crop top. It's burnt orange with a scoop neck and black detail along the hem, and it goes perfectly with my black joggers with the orange stripe. A stray thread has frayed and dangles off the sleeve. I tug it off. I get an allowance from Mum, which I spend mostly online at Bonropa. The clothes there are cheap and tend to fade or twist out of shape very quickly, but they look great for the first few wears. Just because I'm going to be away from civilization for six weeks, it doesn't mean I have to let standards slip.

Mum leads us through a gate to the car park. A woman with a silvery bob steps out from behind the shiniest, sleekest car.

'There she is,' Mum says, sounding relieved.

Gran strides towards us. She's dressed in crisp navy trousers, kitten heels and a silk blouse. She might be old but she knows how to style herself. Unlike Mum, in her shapeless dress and with damp strands of hair plastered over her forehead, Gran looks smart and elegant. Even her nails are perfect: painted a pearly pink that picks out the exact shade of her lipstick.

'Hi.' Mum sounds wary as Gran approaches.

'Hello, love.' Gran leans in to peck Mum on the cheek, then pats Leo on the shoulder and nods at me. The sun glints off the delicate gold chain around her neck. 'It's wonderful to see you all.' I'd forgotten how brisk she is, every movement precise. 'Good journey?'

'Fine,' Mum says, shifting her bulging bag higher up her shoulder. 'Thanks so much for this. I've been so worried about leaving them.' Her gaze drifts to Leo.

'No need for thanks,' says Gran, bristling. 'We're family.'

'Of course. Er, I have to go, I'm afraid,' Mum says. 'Make my connection. Evening drinks on the first night of a conference – the biggest networking opportunity of the weekend.'

A disapproving gleam creeps into Gran's eyes. 'Well, I hope you're going to put on something a little more formal before you start mingling,' she says, sharply. 'And, darling, I'm only saying this because I love you, but you really need to do something about that hair.'

My jaw drops. Way to go with the direct approach, Gran.

There's an awkward silence.

'Right,' mutters Mum. She looks like she wants to say more, but stops herself. Instead, she turns to Leo and pulls him into her arms. Leo submits, even though he's never been a big fan of hugging. 'Be good for Gran and Grandad.' Mum turns to me. 'Don't spend *all* your time on your phone, Maya. Get outside . . . where it's safe, obviously.'

'Bye, Mum,' I say, though what I'm thinking is that Leo spends way more time on his phone than I do.

Leo's bottom lip trembles again.

'Well, no point in long, drawn-out goodbyes,' Gran says.

Mum gives Leo a final kiss, wraps her arms around me

for a short, fierce hug, then turns quickly away. One of the laces on her trainers trails in the dust as she disappears back onto the platform. Leo stares after her, clearly trying hard not to cry.

I feel numb as the reality of this nightmare summer in the middle of nowhere settles like a stone in my guts.

'Come along,' Gran says crisply. 'I need to pop into work.'

Leo and I hurry after her. 'Work?' I ask. 'Aren't we going to your house?'

'As soon as I've checked one thing at the factory.' Gran opens the boot of her shiny car and we dump our luggage inside. 'Leo, you sit in the back. Seat belt on, please. Maya, up front with me.' There's a way she has of speaking which doesn't allow for disagreement. Leo obediently scrambles into the back seat. I hesitate, my hand on the car door.

'In you get, Maya,' Gran urges, sliding elegantly into the driver's seat. 'I'm sure you'll be pleased to hear that we've introduced lots of new green measures at the factory since you were last here.'

'Oh.' I shrug. I barely remember anything about the factory, but the last thing I want is to encourage Gran to talk about it.

'Yes, Peyton Soaps is much more environmentally friendly than it used to be,' Gran says as we head out of the car park. 'I've changed lots of our production methods and made sure *all* our waste water is properly treated and *all* our rubbish is taken to reputable recycling facilities.' She pats the steering wheel. 'I know how important environmental issues are to you young people.'

How patronizing.

'Great,' I say.

'How do you treat waste water?' Leo asks.

'Ah, well,' Gran says, 'there's an interesting process known as flocculation, which . . .'

I stop listening and stare out of the window, feeling more and more depressed. The glass is tinted, which makes the hedges and fields we're speeding past look dull and grey. Ten minutes pass and we don't see so much as another car, let alone a building. Gran is now talking about the history of Peyton Soaps, telling Leo the story I already know: how it was set up as a family business sixty years ago by Gran's father and why it is now one of the biggest employers in the region.

We take the turning for Penwillick. The road narrows as we approach a low bridge.

'We're almost at the factory,' Gran says.

I gaze out, over a glistening stream. It stretches away from the road, towards an expanse of woodland beyond it. A group of five or six people are chatting by the trees.

Most of them are in shadow, but one boy about my age, dressed in shorts and a T-shirt, is standing in a pool of light, his blond hair glinting like a halo. A little girl in a pinafore dress runs over, and starts jumping up and down in front of him.

As we draw closer, the boy looks up. He scowls at the car.

Even though I know he can't see me through the tinted window, I shrink back. Why is he glowering like that?

Gran gives a tut as we drive away, over the bridge.

'I see the eco nutters are out in force today,' she says, a particularly sharp edge to her voice now.

'Eco nutters?' I ask.

'Bunch of hippies who live in Penwillick Wood,' Gran explains. 'Despite my best efforts, they got council permission to build a small community there a few years ago.'

'Why did you object?' I ask, feeling confused. Didn't Gran just say how environmentally friendly her company was?

'I don't want a group of smug, grubby activists camped in my neighbourhood,' she says. 'Who knows what they get up to!' She sighs. 'I lodged a fresh appeal against their community a couple of months ago, but I don't hold out much hope. These days, anything remotely

9

green-sounding gets a pass, no matter how much it costs everyone else.'

'I thought Peyton Soaps was all about being green?' I ask.

'That's completely different,' Gran retorts with a sniff. 'I'm making those changes for the good of the company. Those squatters are *extremists*. Prepared to go to any lengths to get what they want.'

I turn and look out through the back window of the car. The boy is still glaring at us.

A shiver snakes down my spine.

Once over the bridge, the car picks up speed. We pass a telephone box – which is basically the only object that isn't a tree I've seen since we left the station – then Gran takes the next turning on the right.

'Here we are,' she says. A long road leads up to an industrial estate. Gran drives through some gates into a car park then stops by the first building: modern and red-brick, with the sign PEYTON SOAPS in large letters over the door. 'You can both come in with me,' Gran says, stepping out of the car. 'It won't take long.'

Leo scrambles out of the back. I follow more slowly.

'While we're inside,' Gran goes on, 'I expect you'd like to see our state-of-the-art cold saponification vessel.'

'What's that?' Leo asks eagerly.

I roll my eyes.

'It's a cold process soap-making machine,' Gran explains. 'It doesn't use heat, which is much more environmentally friendly than the old methods, though it takes far longer.'

'I think I'll skip that,' I say, feeling sulky.

'Ah, okay.' Gran rests her hand lightly on my shoulder. 'In that case, Maya, you should use the time to find out about your job. I'll—'

'What?' I stare at her. 'What job?'

Gran smiles. 'Your summer job, here at Peyton Soaps,' she says. 'Come on.'

TWO

No *way*. Gran *has* to be kidding. The next few weeks are going to be bad enough without me having to work for the family company as well.

She and Leo are already almost at the main door. I hurry across the tarmac after them.

'Are you serious, Gran?' I squeak. 'About the summer job?'

'Of course.' Gran casts a glance over her shoulder. 'You'll be putting in a shift here from nine till three, every weekday, while you're staying here. Didn't your mother mention it?'

'No.' I stare at her. 'But I—'

'It'll be great experience,' Gran interrupts, charging inside and through the empty reception area. 'For goodness' sake,' she mutters under her breath, 'where on earth is Parvati?' She turns and takes Leo's hand. 'Come on, Leo, put that phone away.'

Leo meekly slides his mobile into his pocket. The two of them disappear through the door beside the reception desk. Irritation twists inside me.

This isn't fair.

I follow Gran and Leo into an open-plan office area. Four back-to-back desks, each set with computer, phone and overflowing in-tray, are positioned in the centre of the room. Only one of them is occupied. A dark-haired man in a crisp, white shirt looks up from his screen. Uncle Harry.

'You're here!' He jumps up and hurries towards us, his arms outstretched and a huge grin on his face.

'Hi, Uncle Harry.' I smile back. It's impossible not to.

Uncle Harry pulls Leo and me into an enormous hug. 'Wow, Leo, you've *grown*.' He releases us and steps back, still grinning.

Leo adjusts his top, looking slightly alarmed. 'Hello,' he says, politely.

'You don't remember me, do you?' Uncle Harry says, nudging Leo on the shoulder.

Leo shakes his head.

Uncle Harry brushes his fringe off his face, but it flops over his forehead again immediately. He turns to me and I'm struck how his eyes are the same hazel colour as Mum's. 'As for you, Maya, I *love* the outfit. *Very* stylish.'

'Thanks.' My cheeks are hot with embarrassment, but underneath I'm beyond delighted that he's noticed. Uncle Harry is as exuberant as Gran is reserved.

'Isn't it great that Maya and Leo are here?' He turns his tanned face to Gran.

I follow his gaze, half expecting Gran to be frowning at his bouncy behaviour. But Gran is smiling fondly at him. 'It is indeed,' she says.

Maybe Mum's right when she says Harry was always Gran's favourite. Born many years after her, Mum claims he's been 'spoilt rotten' his whole life. I don't know about that. As far as I can see, Uncle Harry's just good fun.

'I'm going to take Leo through to the factory,' Gran says. 'Where's Parvati? I want her to show Maya the ropes so she's all ready for work on Monday.'

'About that, Gran . . .' I start.

'Parvati went up to your office a few minutes ago,' Uncle Harry says. 'I can show Maya around while we wait.' His eyes sparkle as he turns to me. 'You'll be helping out with grunt work, which means boring stuff like checking orders and making calls.' He raises his eyebrows. 'But don't worry – you'll get paid!'

'Really?' A small light flickers in the darkness.

'*Plus*, I've got a really interesting project lined up for you too,' Uncle Harry goes on. 'Helping me choose the designs for our new range.'

'What does—?'

'Ah, there's Parvati,' Gran cuts me off. 'At *last*.'

We all turn as a woman with short, black hair hurries towards us.

'Gran,' I say, 'I really—'

'Oh, Ms Peyton, we need to evacuate!' Parvati's voice is breathless with panic. 'Someone just called . . . they said there's a bomb!' She fidgets from side to side, tears welling in her eyes.

Everyone stares at her.

Leo's eyes widen with fear.

'A *bomb*?' Gran frowns. 'Parvati, what *exactly* did they say?'

Parvati blows out a shaky breath. 'The voice was all muffled, like the person was talking through cotton wool . . .' She twists her trembling hands together.

'*And*?' Gran asks.

'They said there's a bomb planted in the building. And it's going to go off in ten minutes. Which is . . . oh, goodness . . . in *nine* minutes.'

I gasp.

'It's got to be a hoax,' Uncle Harry exclaims. 'Why would anyone—?'

'We need to get everyone out.' Gran clutches her forehead. '*Now!*'

'Of course.' Uncle Harry nods, suddenly very serious. He points to the door at the far end of the room. 'I'll clear

15

the factory floor.' He breaks into a run.

As he disappears through the door, Parvati grips Gran's arm: 'What should we do?'

'Maybe you should set off your fire alarm,' I suggest.

Leo nods, huddling closer to my side.

'Yes,' Gran says. 'Parvati, sound the alarm, then get outside. Check everyone off in the car park. I'll call the police myself.'

Parvati nods, then rushes away, back to the reception area. Gran turns and grips my shoulders. 'Maya, take Leo outside.' She points through reception to the main door back to the car park. 'Go out the way we came in. Wait for me by the car. All right?'

'Yes, but—'

'Now!' Gran strides across the room and disappears through the same door that Uncle Harry went through.

I watch her go, my head spinning. It feels like time has slowed. Then, into the silence shoots a piercing alarm. 'Come on, Leo,' I shout over the noise, reaching for his hand. 'Let's get outside.'

There's no reply. No hand meets mine. I look down.

Leo has vanished.

THREE

He was standing here right next to me just a second ago. Until the alarm started to blare out, which he'd have *hated*. Blood rushes to my head. The exit is visible, just a few metres away through the reception area. I race over. The alarm is even louder by the main entrance than it was in the office area. I push open the glass doors. The warm air hits my face. There's no sign of Leo. Across the car park a stream of workers are hurrying out of the factory. Uncle Harry's there, ushering everyone towards Parvati. She's standing by the gates with a clipboard, checking people's names as they pass.

Leo definitely isn't with them.

Panic grips me. The alarm screams out from the speaker above the door, shrill and deafening. I shield my eyes from the sun, and squint across the tarmac to the row of industrial-sized rubbish bins on the other side of the fence. Something moves. A figure in a jacket with the hood up darts away from behind the bins and across the wasteland beyond. I can only see them from the waist up.

I strain my eyes, trying to make out more, but I'm too far away.

Whoever it is, it isn't Leo.

I turn back to the reception area. There's another door, just past the chairs in the waiting area. I yank it open. A short corridor lights up automatically.

'Leo?' My voice echoes off the concrete walls.

No reply. The alarm is still shrieking, making it almost impossible to think. How much time is left of that nine minutes? Six? Five?

How can this be happening?

I race towards the door at the end of the corridor. Leo *must* be on the other side of that.

'Leo!' I yell, shoving the door open. The room beyond fills with light. It's a loading bay, with rows of cluttered shelving along the walls and long, garage-style shutters down to the ground at the far end. The alarm, though still audible, is muffled in here.

'Leo!' I race across the concrete floor, hauling boxes out of my way, searching behind every stack. There's a row of high metal shelving along the far wall. As I run towards it, at last I spot my brother.

He's sitting on the ground at the end of the metal shelves, hunched over his skinny knees, his palms covering his ears.

18

I fill up with a mixture of exasperation and relief. 'There you are!'

This time he hears me. Looks up. 'Maya!' he says, his hands still over his ears. 'It was too loud.'

I race over and grab his arm. 'Come on!' I shout, yanking him upright. 'Come *on*, Leo, we need to get out of here.' I tug him after me, running out of the loading bay and back along the corridor into reception. We fly through the glass doors, tearing across the car park towards Gran and Harry, who are checking behind the parked cars.

'Maya! Leo!' They sound desperate. 'Where are you?'

'Gran!' I shout.

Gran turns, her face filling with relief as Leo and I run towards her. As she draws us into her arms, the 'nee-naw' of distant sirens rises, mingling with the blaring alarm.

'Where on earth were you? Why didn't you go where I told you, when I told you?' she says, crouching down so she's level with Leo. He stares down at his toes.

'It was my fault,' I say quickly.

Gran shoots a sharp look at me, then sighs. She smiles gently at Leo. 'Important thing is, you're both safe,' she says.

As she speaks, a fire engine roars into the car park. A firefighter jumps down, waving his arms.

'Everyone back!' he shouts.

Gran ushers Leo and me towards the gate. Soon everyone is standing well away from the building, behind a cordon. The firefighter speaks briefly to Harry and Gran, then runs off, leaving us huddled together.

'Does the alarm go off a lot?' Leo asks.

Gran gives him a trembly-mouthed smile. 'Normally only for fire drills.' She glances at me and Harry. 'We've never had a bomb threat before.'

People swarm around us: staff from Peyton Soaps, I'm guessing. Leo and I are the only children. Everyone speaks at once, their voices full of fear. Feeling dazed, I catch snatches of their conversations:

'Who would do this—?'

'Who spoke to them—?'

'How much warning did they give—?'

Leo's hands are over his ears again. He takes one away to tug at my sleeve.

'This is it,' he says solemnly. 'The ten minutes are up.'

FOUR

We turn to face the factory.

Nothing happens.

We wait, the warm sun on our faces. Nobody speaks.

After a moment, Leo looks up at Gran. 'Where's the explosion?'

'I told you it was a hoax,' Uncle Harry says, crossing his arms.

'So there isn't a real bomb?' I ask, relieved.

'The firefighters will check – we have to be completely sure,' Gran says.

'Either way, they're not going to let us back into the building for hours.' Uncle Harry groans. 'We'll lose the whole day of production.'

'Why would anyone want to scare us like this?' Parvati asks, her voice shaky.

'I don't know,' Gran says heavily.

There's an awkward pause, then Uncle Harry rubs his hands together and turns to me and Leo. 'Well, this is quite a first day for you two, isn't it?' he says, injecting a more cheerful note into his voice.

'That's right,' Parvati says quickly, copying his fake cheery tone. She smiles. 'It's really nice to meet you, even under these awful circumstances.'

Leo stares blankly at them.

I nod, uncertain of what to say. I hate it when adults pretend that everything's all right when it clearly isn't. Do they really think we won't realize that a workplace bomb – real or not – is as serious and scary as it gets?

Gran clears her throat as if she's about to speak, but stops as a police car, its lights flashing, arrives. A uniformed officer jumps out. She looks around, spots Gran and beckons her over.

'Ms Peyton!' she calls.

Gran hurries across to the policewoman, Uncle Harry at her side. Leo and I are left with Parvati.

'How did that police officer know Gran's name?' Leo asks.

'Your gran is the owner of the factory, ' Parvati explains. 'And everyone knows the Peyton name around here.'

'Do they?' I ask, surprised.

'It's not just the company, it's your gran. She's always been pretty forward-thinking.'

'Really? How?' I frown.

'Well, it might not seem such a big deal to us nowadays,

but she kept her own name when she got married *and* she insisted on passing it on to your mum and your uncle too.' Parvati smiles. 'I guess your mum made the same choice when she passed it on to you and your brother.'

I nod, unwilling to admit that actually my parents were never married and that none of us have seen my dad since Leo was born.

The police set up another cordon, moving us further away from the building. They turn off the fire alarm and the sudden silence is almost spooky. As we're ushered further back behind the tape, Gran and Uncle Harry come over with the policewoman.

'We're almost certain you're right about it being a hoax, Mr Peyton,' the policewoman is saying, 'but we still need to finish our inspection and check your CCTV.' She glances up at the cameras positioned along the front of the building.

'Excuse me,' I stammer. All eyes turn in my direction. 'I don't know if this is important or not, but when I was looking for Leo I saw someone across the road, behind those big bins.' I point to the wasteland opposite. 'They were running towards the wood.'

'Towards the wood?' Gran exchanges a meaningful look with Uncle Harry.

The officer asks me for a description and I explain that

I didn't see a face and it was too far away even to tell whether the figure was male or female. 'Sorry,' I add.

'No, that's very helpful, thank you.' The officer flips her notebook shut, then strides away.

Gran turns to Uncle Harry. 'Perhaps you'd take Leo and Maya home?' she asks. 'I need to have a word with the rest of the staff. And the police may have more questions.'

'Of course.' Harry heads off first to ask one of the officers if it's okay to fetch his car from the car park.

Gran kisses us each on our forehead, then walks over to the big huddle of workers a bit further along the cordon.

Leo and I are left with Parvati. I fidget from foot to foot.

'You did well earlier, Maya. Leo is lucky to have you looking out for him.' Parvati smiles. 'I was supposed to be showing you around today, though I guess that'll have to wait until Monday now.'

Monday. Oh yes. Instead of having a holiday, I'm going to be expected to work.

At least I'll be earning money, which means more clothes. Last time I shopped at Barata, I got a new pair of joggers, two crop tops and some flats, all for £15. Imagine what I'll be able to buy with an actual salary!

A honking sound erupts as Uncle Harry draws up on the other side of the cordon. He's waving from a shiny red sports car, the roof down. 'All aboard!' he shouts, beckoning us forward.

'Whoa, that's a Mercedes Benz Roadster,' says Leo with an enthusiastic grin. 'Cool!'

Uncle Harry glances in Parvati's direction. Is he hoping to impress her with his sports car? Parvati blushes and looks away.

'Come on, Maya!' Leo shouts, already scrambling into the back seat of Uncle Harry's car. I spot his bag on top of my suitcase. Uncle Harry waves me over again. Everyone is looking as I slip under the cordon and make my way, a little self-consciously, to the front passenger seat, where I sink low into the soft leather. A second later, Uncle Harry revs the engine – probably louder than he needs to – and we speed off.

Uncle Harry chats away for the whole of the short journey, answering Leo's questions about his car and pointing out the primary school in Penwillick where he and Mum went when they were kids.

'Not that we were there at the same time,' Uncle Harry adds, 'your mum being *so* much older than me.'

'Ten years and two months older,' Leo says from the back.

'Exactly.' Uncle Harry slaps his hand on the steering wheel, just like Gran did earlier. A minute later we come to a turning marked PRIVATE ROAD. Uncle Harry drives us along the tree-lined track, the bright blue sky huge overhead.

In spite of all my earlier resentments, my heart lifts as we turn into the broad driveway of Gran and Grandad's house: a large, modern building with huge windows. There are white roses climbing up the walls and all shapes and colours of flowers arranged in tidy rows under the windows. I don't remember this house at all – I haven't been here since I was tiny – but I can see straight away that it's like Gran herself: stylish and neat.

It's the same in the hall, where a single pot plant sits elegantly on a polished-wood table. There's a coat stand next to the door, with two pegs free – for me and Leo, presumably. Uncle Harry points out Gran and Grandad's bedroom, explaining Grandad can't manage the stairs now, then leads us to the back of the house, where the hall opens into a big, airy kitchen on one side and what looks like a living room on the other. Everything is carefully ordered – the exact opposite of the jumble and chaos at home with Mum.

Leo runs ahead of me, into the living room.

I hurry after him. It's a square, comfortable room, with three squishy-looking sofas set around a modern stone fireplace. But it's not the room that takes my breath away.

It's the view from the window.

FIVE

I stare through the living-room window, my mouth gaping.

Gran and Grandad's house must be built on a hill, because the back of it is far higher up than the front. Immediately outside is a small, neatly manicured back garden, and beyond and below that, stretching out into the distance, is the sea. The turquoise water glistens like a silk scarf scattered with sequins.

'Wow!' I gasp.

'Did you know that water appears blue because it absorbs the colours in the red part of the light spectrum?' Leo asks, his head tilted to one side. 'That leaves the colours in the blue part, which is what we see.'

'Right,' I say, still gazing through the window.

'Pretty cool, eh?' Uncle Harry says proudly from the doorway. 'There are steps straight down to the beach.'

'Seriously?' For the first time since I arrived I find myself smiling.

'Let's go and find your grandad,' suggests Uncle Harry.

We follow him through the patio doors and out to the back garden. The lawn is soft underfoot and surrounded by perfectly ordered beds full of colourful flowers. I hurry to the hedge at the end of the garden. A set of steep stone steps leads down to a gate, with the sandy shore beyond.

A throb of excitement thrills through me.

'Hello, there!'

I spin around. Grandad is limping across the lawn towards us, leaning heavily on his stick. He looks much older than I remember from our occassional video chats. Leo hangs shyly back, leaving it to me to go over and let Grandad hug me.

His shirt smells slightly musty as he squeezes me tight.

'Good to see you, Maya. I can't believe how grown-up you've got.' Grandad turns to Leo and gives him an affectionate smile, tousling his hair. 'And you too, young man. But how come you're back so early? I wasn't expecting you for another half-hour or so.' He looks at Uncle Harry.

'There was a bomb at the factory,' Leo says solemnly.

'What?' Grandad's watery eyes open wide.

'A bomb *scare*,' Uncle Harry clarifies. 'Just time-wasters with nothing better to do. The police and fire service are there now.'

'That's *terrible*!' Grandad takes a step towards the house. 'I must call your gran.'

'She's in the thick of it there, Dad,' Uncle Harry points out.

'Right, right,' Grandad says. 'I'll call a bit later. So who made this threat then?'

'It was an anonymous call,' I tell him.

Grandad shakes his head.

'I bet it was those crazy hippies from Penwillick Wood,' Uncle Harry says, a bitter note creeping into his voice. 'Maya here saw someone running away in that direction soon after the call was made.'

'I couldn't see enough to describe them though,' I add.

Grandad frowns. 'Surely the Penwillick Wood group wouldn't do such a thing. They're peaceniks, against violence of all kinds.'

Harry snorts. 'As far as *I'm* concerned, they're a bunch of lunatics – all eat-your-own-crystals and bring down the system, while still being happy of course to use the schools and hospitals the rest of us pay our taxes for.'

'Don't they pay too?' Leo asks.

'That's not the—' Harry starts.

'Ah, well, let's change the subject,' Grandad interrupts, giving Uncle Harry a meaningful look. He turns to me and Leo. 'I'm sorry you kids had such a dramatic start to your holiday. Now, I expect you'll be wanting some tea?'

'What's that for?' Leo points to a round, windowless

hut in the corner of the garden. Its glossy green paint shines in the sunlight.

Grandad's eyes twinkle. 'That, young man, is my astronomy hut. What do you know about the planets?'

'I know lots of things,' Leo says. 'Like Venus and Mercury don't have moons and the wind on Neptune can blow faster than the speed of sound.'

'Goodness.' Grandad looks impressed.

'Have you got a telescope?' Leo asks.

'I have indeed.' Grandad chuckles. 'Shall I show you and Maya?'

'Er, thanks, but science isn't really my thing,' I say.

'How about I take the bags up and show Maya her room?' Harry suggests. 'We'll be back down for some tea in a few minutes.'

I throw him a grateful glance. Grandad agrees, and I watch him shuffle off towards the hut, leaning on his stick again. Leo trots along at his side. I follow Uncle Harry back indoors. After he's fetched our bags from his car, he leads me up to the first floor.

'You're in here, Maya.' Uncle Harry sets my suitcase down beside the door at the top of the stairs. 'Used to be your mum's room.' Just then, his phone rings and he wanders across the landing to take the call.

I turn the handle and go inside the bedroom. A

window runs along the whole of the wall on the right, with an even more incredible view of the sea than there was downstairs. On the far wall stands a massive fitted wardrobe that looks easily big enough for all the clothes I've brought with me – plus the ones I'm planning to buy with my new salary. Between the window and the wardrobe is a double bed with brass railings: definitely the biggest, most glamorous bed I'll ever have slept in.

Uncle Harry reappears in the doorway. 'Good news from the factory. The police and fire brigade have confirmed the call was a hoax.' He makes a face. 'Even so, we can't resume production today. So, what do you think of your room? You can see all the way to Penwillick Wood from the window.'

'It's perfect,' I say. 'I don't understand why Mum didn't bring us here more often.'

'Ah well . . .' Uncle Harry taps the side of his nose, as if to indicate there's some secret explanation for this. 'Once she'd left, I don't think she felt much like looking back.' I want to ask him what he means, but before I have the chance Uncle Harry says: 'I'm going to drop Leo's bag over there.' He points to the door at the end of the landing. 'That's *my* old room.'

'Where do you sleep now?' I ask.

'Next door.' He grins. 'We had the garage converted

into a flat for me. Right then, I'll leave you to get sorted.'

Left alone, I curl up on the long, deep window seat and check my phone. Mum has texted to ask how we are. I text back that we're fine. I decide not to tell her about the bomb scare. She'll just freak out. I sit back against a couple of silk cushions, trying to find the best angle for a picture of the distant sea.

I can see more of the beach from up here on the first floor. To the left, it widens into the curve of a bay, bounded by high cliffs. Family groups are dotted across the sand at the far end. That must be close to Penwillick town centre. To the right, the beach is more-or-less deserted, narrowing and twisting away until it's no longer visible, the view of it blocked by dense trees. Presumably that's Penwillick Wood: home to the eco group Uncle Harry and Gran are convinced are behind the hoax bomb scare.

I take a picture of the view, then unpack my things. It's too hot for the joggers I'm wearing, so I change into denim shorts with a daisy over the pocket, and team them with a summery vest top with tiny daisies embroidered over the straps. I ease my hot feet out of my trainers and slip on a pair of bright yellow flipflops, then change my earrings for big yellow plastic hoops.

I check my reflection. My mousy brown hair falls in a straight line down to my shoulders and my eyes are a kind of sludgy blue-grey. I'd like a bit more of a tan on my arms and legs and but otherwise I think I look okay, albeit very ordinary. I take another picture, this time a selfie. I'll post both pics later.

With a last look in the mirror, I make my way downstairs. Grandad has laid out a plate of cakes and sandwiches on the kitchen table, and Leo is already tucking in enthusiastically.

I take a currant bun and Grandad sets glasses of milk in front of us. I wouldn't normally dream of drinking a glass of milk, but somehow, here in this smart, comfortable kitchen, with the clear sky and glistening sea outside, it feels like exactly what I want.

Uncle Harry is sitting at the kitchen table, busily tapping away at a laptop. Grandad asks some more questions about our journey, then he and Leo disappear outside again.

Once they're gone, Harry looks up. 'Let's get to work!' He smoothes his dark, wavy hair off his face and turns his computer towards me. A grid of seashell images is on the screen.

'Your first job for Peyton Soaps,' he says with a smile, 'is to pick out a shell we can use as branding for our new range. We're starting with soap, but eventually we're planning to broaden out to include handwash, moisturizers and shampoo bars. We're calling it Peyton

Seashell and it's aimed at teens and younger women.' He wrinkles his nose. 'Not sure about the name, if I'm honest, but it fits with our brand.' He indicates the screen. 'You up for this? We need a shell that says, "fresh", "youthful" and "stylish".'

I stare at him. 'You want *me* to choose?'

'Come up with a shortlist of three for me to have a look at,' Uncle Harry says. 'I'll be briefing the design agency next week. I want to give them a proper steer, and anything *you* like should get us in the right ball park, I reckon.' He grins. 'You've got a good eye, Maya – anyone can see that from the way you put your outfits together.'

Trying not to show how pleased I am, I settle myself at the table. 'What's your job at Peyton, exactly?' I ask.

'I'm head of marketing and product development,' Uncle Harry says.

I glance sideways at him. 'What about Parvati – what does she do?'

'Parvati's the office manager and basically Gran's PA. She's amazing, actually. Keeps Peyton Soaps running.' He sighs, though I'm not sure if it's because he's pining for Parvati or feels sympathy for all the hard work she has to do. Uncle Harry stands up. 'I'll see you later. Gotta get back to the office, see what's going on.' He saunters off, whistling to himself as he goes.

I turn my attention to the screen in front of me. I scan the shell images . . . There are so many of them, it's overwhelming. A sliver of anxiety curls itself around my earlier happiness. Maybe Uncle Harry is expecting too much of me. I have no idea how to decide what would or wouldn't look good on a skincare range.

After a few minutes, I close the laptop. Perhaps the beach will give me some inspiration. Outside in the back garden, Grandad and Leo are examining a plant with spiky red leaves. I call out as I pass that I'm going for a quick walk, and head for the stone steps.

I half expect Grandad to stop me, or at the very least ask questions about where I'm going, but he simply waves, calling out that I shouldn't be too long.

The bottom steps are shrouded in shade from the thick hedges on either side. The bolt on the wooden gate slides back easily and I slip through to the footpath beyond. The wind is stronger out here – a warm, salty breeze that whips across my cheeks. I cross over the grassy area that leads down to the beach. The sea sucks and swishes over the sand. A pair of seagulls squawk and swoop overhead.

I walk along the shore, stopping every now and then to examine a shell. Penwillick Wood is visible in the distance. Curious, I head towards the trees. The sun warms my face as I pad across the compacted sand. After a while, the beach curves deeply away, the sea suddenly distant, and the sand under my feet becomes softer and grassier.

I reach the wood after another fifteen minutes or so. There's no sign of the eco camp. I guess it must be much further into the trees. The branches above rustle in the wind. A twig snaps, sending a shiver down my spine. I take a step into the wood. The air here is cooler, fresh with the scent of damp earth.

Another light, snapping sound. The skin on the back of my neck prickles.

'Hello?' I say. 'Is someone there?'

For a second there's no answer, and then – from behind a tree – a figure steps out into view.

It's the boy with blond hair I saw glaring at us earlier, on the drive from the station.

He's still scowling.

SIX

Close up, I can see that the boy is about my age. His hair, which shone like a golden halo when I saw him earlier, is, in fact, a tousled mix of blond and caramel streaks. He's wearing shorts to his knees, and a faded T-shirt that reflects exactly the pale green of his eyes.

My heart thuds. 'Hi,' I say, self-consciously smoothing down my top. 'I'm Maya.'

We stare at each other. There's an awkwardness underlying the boy's scowl. Perhaps he's just shy. Not hostile, like I'd thought.

'I'm Bear,' he says at last. 'Are you here on holiday?'

'Not exactly.' I'm about to tell him about Gran, then I remember her saying how she'd tried to stop the eco community from living in Penwillick Wood. Maybe I won't mention my connection to Peyton Soaps just yet. 'I'm here for the summer.'

'And yet not on holiday? How mysterious.' Bear grins and it's like the sun coming out from behind a cloud. I can't help but smile back. He is seriously attractive, with those green eyes and clear, tanned skin.

'What about you?' I ask.

'I live through there.' He indicates the wood behind him.

'In . . . in the eco camp?'

'You've heard of it?' An expression – part proud, part wary – crosses Bear's face. 'It's actually called the Harmony Earth Group,' he explains. 'My family set it up.'

'Really?' A million questions flood my brain.

Bear nods. 'Lots of people around here think we're, like, really extreme, that we want to make trouble, but we're totally peaceful. We just try and co-exist in harmony with the planet. You know, living off the land, being sustainable. We still do plenty of normal stuff.'

'Do you go to school?'

'Actually we do home school,' Bear explains, his voice growing more defensive. 'But it doesn't make us weird.'

'I didn't say it did.'

There's a pause, the only sounds the sea swooshing in the distance and the branches above our heads swaying in the breeze.

'Sorry.' Bear hesitates. 'It's just sometimes people act like we're evil just for wanting to live off-grid.' I flush, thinking of how both Gran and Uncle Harry had suggested exactly that earlier. 'If . . . if you're interested, I could show you around?'

Before I can reply, the sound of twigs snapping and crunching fills the air. I glance up. A girl, a similar age to us, and with wild, dark curls, is stomping towards us. She stops about a metre away, hands on her hips, and turns to Bear.

'Who's this?' she demands, a haughty tilt to her chin. 'What does she want?'

My jaw drops at her rudeness. The girl scans me up and down. She's tall and slim and dressed in a faded cotton jumpsuit and canvas sneakers. Despite the sneer on her face, she's undeniably pretty.

'Don't be like that, Rowan,' Bear says. 'This is Maya. She's here for the summer.'

Rowan's angry eyes rest on my face. Her lips are a perfect bow shape, her eyes a bright cornflower blue. Is this Bear's girlfriend? She certainly seems like the kind of girl boys would *want* for a girlfriend. That jumpsuit is saggy and shapeless, but she still looks like a supermodel in it. I'm suddenly horribly aware that my own outfit, with its matchy-matchy daisies and loud plastic earrings, must look overthought and fussy.

'I was just asking about your camp,' I say. 'And, to answer your question, I don't *want* anything.'

Rowan sniffs, looking at me with contempt. 'What an emmet.'

I frown. I have no idea what an emmet is, but I'm not going to let the girl know that. Bear senses my confusion.

'Ro just means you're a tourist,' he says apologetically. 'Emmet is Cornish for holidaymaker.'

'Actually I have a summer job.' I immediately wish I hadn't said anything.

'Really?' Bear asks.

'We have to go.' Rowan turns to him. 'We're foraging this afternoon, and if you don't come now, Bear, we'll be late.'

Bear shrugs, apparently unbothered. 'So, Maya, would you like to see the camp? Maybe tomorrow?'

'Sure,' I say. 'Er, you can message me with the address or whatever.'

Rowan gives a sarcastic laugh. 'Bear and I don't use mobiles,' she says scornfully, 'so I'm afraid he can't give you his *number*.' She puts a big emphasis on the last word. I can feel my face reddening.

'Stop it, Ro.' Bear's cheeks are pinking too. He fixes me with his clear, pale-green eyes. 'Just meet me here at midday, Maya.'

'Okay.' I smile back.

'Come *on*, Bear,' Rowan snaps. 'You're not getting *me* into trouble.'

'See you tomorrow.' A final smile and Bear turns away.

He slips into the trees. I watch him go, struck by the graceful way he moves.

Rowan leans in, her face too close. It takes all my nerve not to shrink back, but I hold her mean, hate-filled gaze.

'Stay away from us,' she hisses at me. 'Stay away from Bear or you'll be sorry.'

Before I can speak, she turns on her heel and stomps off, crashing through the wood as loudly as Bear was silent. I stare after her, into the trees. Why would she threaten me like that? Bear *asked* me to come visit him tomorrow.

I turn away and, as I walk along the beach, the sun dips behind a white, fluffy cloud. It's low in the sky, which means I must have been out here longer than I thought. I hurry back to Gran's.

Leo and Grandad are chatting away on the steps of the astronomy hut and I wave and scuttle past them, into the house. Gran is in the kitchen, preparing salad. She's changed out of her smart trousers and silk blouse into palazzo pants and a soft cotton T-shirt. Even in casual clothes she looks elegant, her silvery bob hanging in a sharp line just above her shoulders.

'There you are, Maya,' she says as I walk in. 'I was worried you'd got lost.'

I shake my head. 'I just took a walk along the beach.'

Gran nods, slicing a tomato. 'It's fine for you to go on

the beach, but do be careful of the sea at high tide if you decide to go swimming.'

'I will,' I say, thinking that I'll definitely be wanting a bit more of a tan before I venture into my swimsuit.

'And I'd like you to avoid Penwillick Wood, please,' Gran says, looking up from the chopping board.

'Oh?' The wood is where I've arranged to meet Bear tomorrow. 'Why?'

'The police agree that the bomb scare was likely the work of the activists who live there. The person you saw running away from the factory, not only were they heading towards the eco camp . . .' she pauses, 'but certain members of that camp have a *record of violence*.'

I stare at her. 'Seriously?'

She nods. 'The police officer told me. They were part of a recent protest up north that turned extremely nasty. Two people ended up in hospital, and apparently someone from the camp was arrested.'

Can that really be true?

'They spout all this idealistic nonsense about "living off the land", but under the surface they're revolutionary extremists.' Gran shakes her head sorrowfully. 'Plus, of course, they have a vendetta against me because I'm appealing against their right to live in the wood. It all adds up.'

'But there's no proof,' I say, 'about the bomb scare, I mean.'

'Not yet.' Gran picks up a handful of spring onions and lines them up carefully on the chopping board.

'And . . . and . . . Grandad said they were *against* violence.'

'Mmm.' Gran sniffs. 'Well, he's a great one for never thinking badly of anyone.' She looks up at me. 'What gets me is that we've made so much effort at Peyton Soaps over the past couple of years to reduce our carbon footprint. We use highly environmentally friendly production processes *and* pay over the odds to have our waste dealt with in a sustainable way – not just the waste water but *all* the packaging. And look where it gets us!'

'At least there wasn't a real bomb,' I stammer.

'No.' Gran meets my eyes. 'But there could have been.'

A chill runs down my spine. Earlier, Bear was adamant that local people keep making assumptions about them that aren't true.

What if he was lying?

'Have you ever visited the eco camp?' I ask.

'Why would I do that?' Gran snorts with derision. 'Bunch of idiots. I know some of them mean well, but they seem to think the solution to the climate crisis is going back to the stone age. Of course I sympathize with their environmental concerns, but opting out of real life is no solution. And this latest thing with the bomb scare . . .' She looks at me intently. 'That must have been terrifying for you. Are you all right?'

'I'm fine,' I say, honestly.

'Did you meet anyone out on your walk?'

I hesitate. This is my chance to tell Gran about Bear. But if I do that, she'll certainly forbid me from seeing him again.

'No,' I say, 'I didn't meet anyone.'

SEVEN

I've only been in Cornwall a few hours and already *nothing* is like I imagined it would be. There are so many thoughts whirring round my head, I don't imagine I'll ever get to sleep but, in fact, I drop off quickly, soothed by the sound of rolling waves through the open window.

I wake the next morning with a start, to find the sun streaming in through drawn curtains and Leo hopping from foot to foot at the end of my bed. 'We're going to explore the rock pools,' he says. 'Me and Grandad. He reckons there's a good chance we'll find a double-headed jellyfish on a stalk *and* a hairy hermit crab. Maybe even a snake pipefish.'

I stare at him, bleary-eyed. 'What's the time?'

'Nearly half past eleven.'

'*What?*' I sit bolt upright. I only have half an hour before I'm supposed to meet Bear.

'Gran said earlier that I had to wait, but now it's time you should wake up,' Leo chatters on. 'If you want, you can come with me and Grandad?'

'I can't,' I say. 'Sorry, Leo, I'm . . . I've got plans.'

'Plans to do what?'

'Sunbathing,' I lie. 'Reading a book on the beach.'

Leo wrinkles his nose. 'But you never read books.'

He's right, of course. Leo himself reads non-stop, but, to me, books are like slow internet connections where you can only open one screen at a time.

'You're meeting someone, aren't you?' Leo stares intently at me.

Sometimes, I swear it's like he's psychic.

'No!' I lie. 'Now, go – I need to get dressed!' and I shoo him away.

As Leo pads downstairs, I fling open my wardrobe and scan the row of tops and dresses and cut-offs. What should I wear? I need something boho and countrified. Something that will fit in at the eco camp. All my normal athleisure clothes suddenly look too slick and 'city-ish'. At last I decide on one of my few skirts, with tiers in various shades of blue, plus a plain white top. I slip on a pair of strappy blue sandals, then switch to a pair of trainers. I'm going to have to walk through a wood so I don't want to be sliding out of my shoes looking like – what did that Rowan person call me – an emmet?

I step back and study myself in the mirror. Not bad, I think: I've kept it successfully simple, with a dash of eco-friendly hippyishness. I definitely want to keep my make-up and accessories low-key too, so I just flick a little mascara on my eyelashes, then select a small crossbody bag for my lip gloss, mobile and the spare keys Gran has given me.

It's ten to twelve by the time I'm done. I hurry downstairs, grabbing an apple from the bowl in the kitchen before rushing out to the back garden. Gran and Grandad are pottering by the flower beds, while Leo examines the petals of an enormous sunflower.

'Where are you off to, Maya?' Gran calls out as I fly past.

I stop. 'Just a walk,' I say, then remembering my fib to Leo I add: 'I'm really into this book. I . . . er . . . I thought I'd read it on the beach.'

Grandad nods.

'A book?' Gran says, peering at my tiny crossbody bag. 'Where is it?'

I gulp. I might have guessed nothing would get past her. 'On my phone,' I lie.

Gran stares at me as if I'm mad. Grandad lets out a low chuckle. 'That told you,' he says, nudging Gran in the ribs.

'Okay then,' Gran says, now laughing herself. 'Just be careful. And make sure you're back for your mum's video call at three thirty.'

Released, I hurry across the garden and let myself out through the gate. Moments later I'm scurrying along the beach. Mum would have wanted to know exactly where I was going. Gran and Grandad, I realize, treat me more like a grown-up, trusting me to look after myself.

I can see Bear, waiting by the trees, long before I reach him. He smiles shyly as I approach. He's wearing long shorts again and another faded T-shirt. There's something about the way he stands, leaning against a tree, that I can't take my eyes off. That streaky-blond hair – which is clearly natural – looks like a set of Instagram-influencer highlights. But it's the intense way he looks at me that really unsettles me.

'I wasn't sure you'd come,' he says.

'Ah. Well, I did,' I say, trying to sound nonchalant.

We make our way through the trees. It's cool in here and shady, light filtering in through the leaves. The only sound is the occasional rustle of foliage and the distant whoosh of the sea. We fall silent as we walk. I have a million questions for Bear – how he lives, what he eats, how he survives without a phone and what his home-schooling is like – but I don't know how to ask any of them without sounding stupid or, worse, making it seem that I think he's weird for being so different.

After about fifteen minutes we reach a large clearing.

Two wooden huts stand opposite each other.

'I live there,' Bear says, pointing to the larger hut. Yellow curtains flutter at its open window. A tarpaulin covered with bits of machinery is spread on the ground on one side of it. On the other side is a huge solar panel. 'Our dunny is further back.'

'Dunny?' I wrinkle my nose. 'What's that?'

'Toilet,' Bear says. 'Dunny is what Mum calls it. It's a composting toilet, so there's no smell.' He points to a narrow path at the back of his hut. 'It's up there. We have a couple of showers too. There's a filtration system for the water and we heat it with a solar panel and this thermo-siphon-based—' He stops, clearly noticing my jaw gaping. 'What?'

'I . . . er . . . nothing. It's just . . . you don't have a bathroom in your house?' I can't get the disbelief out of my voice.

'Nope.' Bear grins. 'D'you want to see inside?'

I nod and he leads me into the hut. After the glare of the sun, my eyes take a second to adjust to the shade inside. I don't know what I was expecting, but somehow I'm surprised by how spacious and homely it is: the rough wooden walls and floor are covered with colourful fabrics and rugs, with a large brown sofa positioned under a long window. There's a kitchen area at the end, where a round table surrounded by four chairs is set with a small bowl of apples.

I'm just thinking how different from Gran's modern designer house the place is, when the door on the other side of the kitchen creaks open.

EIGHT

'Is that you, Bear?' A woman with long red hair, her dungarees rolled up to the knees, walks into the kitchen. She sees me and stops, eyes widening in surprise. 'Oh, hello. I'm Val, Bear's mum.'

'Hi,' I say. 'Maya.'

'We met near the beach,' explains Bear, his cheeks pinking. 'Er, Maya just wanted to see the camp.'

'No worries!' His mum smiles. 'Nice to meet you.' There's a twang to her accent. I'm guessing she's from Australia but, before I can ask, a little girl appears from behind her. The same girl I saw laughing with Bear yesterday near the bridge, but dressed now in pink shorts and a tie-dye T-shirt.

'This is Skye,' Bear says. 'My sister.'

Skye gazes shyly at me. Her red hair – the same colour as her mum's – is tied in two bunches that stick out over her ears.

'Hello, Skye,' I say.

My gaze drifts around the kitchen, taking in the low

metal stove with two kettles perched on top of it, the countertop ranged with bottles and jars. There's a sink under the window, but instead of a metal tap rising up over it, a large glass water butt is set to the side.

'Would you like some water?' Bear's mum asks.

I nod. 'Yes, please.'

As she turns on the water butt tap, my eyes wander to the laptop propped next to a rough wooden cupboard.

'You have a computer?' I ask, surprised.

'Sure,' Bear says matter-of-factly. 'We charge it through solar power.'

'Most of our energy comes from the sun,' Bear's mum says, offering me a glass of water. I take a tentative sip.

'It's okay,' she says, laughing. 'We get water from the local stream, then purify it. We just have what we need to drink in the houses, a bit more in the communal kitchen. Everyone takes turns fetching it.'

'We take turns with everything,' Skye adds.

I nod, feeling overwhelmed. I've never been anywhere remotely like this.

'Did you explain how Harmony Earth Group started?' Bear's mum asks him.

'No, Mum, I don't think—'

'Of course she's interested,' his mum says, apparently reading both my mind and her son's. She gestures me to the table and I sit down, feeling slightly dazed by the difference between my world and the one I've just wandered into. Bear's mum is different from other adults I've met, too: gentle, but strong. I can't explain how, but she seems to change the air around her, making the atmosphere calmer.

'I'm originally from Perth in Australia,' Bear's mum explains, sitting down opposite me. Skye hovers at her side, watching me with saucer eyes. 'I came here as a student, fell pregnant with Bear and then Skye – their dads were never much in the picture – and then, a few years ago, I met Drina.'

'Drina?' I glance at Bear as he takes the seat next to mine.

'She's, like, my step-mum,' he explains.

'Before we met, Drina made lots of money in finance, but was really disillusioned with that world. We were both – we *are* both – passionate about finding a sustainable way to live. Soon after we met, Drina used the money she'd saved to buy this patch of woodland at auction. There were already eight huts on the land. We decided to turn them into proper homes, to set up our own community.'

'That's amazing,' I say.

'It wasn't easy.' Bear's mum makes a face. 'We had to fight endless objections from local businesses and community groups. In fact, one local business is *still* trying to get us out. The owner launched an appeal against our being here just a few months ago.'

'Oh.' Heat creeps up my cheeks. She's talking about Gran.

Bear's mum sighs. 'I don't understand why we upset people so much. We're not a threat to anyone, we just live in a different way.'

'Right.' Trying to cover up my awkwardness, I ask: 'How many people are here?'

'At the moment, nine permanent – that's adults. Plus seven children. One of the huts is a communal longhouse, a kitchen-cum-living-space, but otherwise we live in families. We have a hut for visitors too, which we rent out for a month at a time, so that other people can experience the way we live.'

'So . . . so are you totally cut off from the outside world?'

Bear laughs.

'Not at all,' his mum explains. 'The teacher who runs our home school helps out at a food bank at weekends and we have two carpenters and a gardener who all work for regular clients as well as within the camp. Plus there's John. He's a solicitor; well, he's retired, but he still does volunatry legal work all across Cornwall. I'm a yoga teacher. No one has much money, but then we're not about having lots of money. We're about living in a sustainable way, in harmony with the Earth.' She pauses, then reaches behind her for a basket of rolls. She sets them on the table, indicating I should take one.

'Where are you from, Maya?'

'London,' I say, tucking into the bread. It's delicious: soft and fresh and nutty. Bear takes a roll for himself, then fetches a slab of cheese. He cuts me a slice and I eat hungrily.

Skye walks across the kitchen to where a large, colourful crayon-drawing of a garden is propped up against a cupboard.

'I did this,' she says proudly.

'It's great,' I say, swallowing a mouthful of bread and cheese.

Skye moves the picture closer to the table. My eye is caught by the thick black print on the poster underneath, now exposed:

POLLUTERS MUST PAY!

I set down my roll, feeling troubled.

'Are you here on holiday?' Bear's mum asks me.

I can't look away from the words on the poster. They read like a threat.

'It's for a placard,' Bear says, following my gaze. 'We

do that sometimes . . . go on protests. You know, like climate change marches.'

'Have you ever been on one?' Skye asks, big-eyed.

I shake my head.

'We try to hold companies to account,' his mum goes on. 'If they spill oil, we demand they should clear it up, just like they shouldn't dump raw sewage in the sea or industrial waste on our beaches. It's all we can do: ask them to take responsibility for their actions.'

I nod, feeling relieved.

Skye shuffles from foot to foot. She holds up her crayon-drawing. It's full of flowers in bright, primary colours. 'This is what our vegetable garden would look like if it had more flowers,' she says with a shy smile.

I smile back. 'It's lovely.'

Skye beams, dimples appearing in her cheeks.

'So, Maya,' Bear's mum says, 'I was just asking if you are here on holiday?'

I stare at her, then at Bear. No way can I tell them the truth, that I'm connected to Gran and to Peyton Soaps. 'Sort of,' I say. 'Mum and I are here for the summer. My mum's sick, she can't work at the moment.' The lie blurts out of me and I flush with shame.

Where the hell did that come from?

'Oh, that must be hard.' Bear's mum's voice fills with

sympathy. I can feel Bear's eyes on me. Skye's too.

My guts twist, guiltily. 'It's fine. With my mum, I mean. She's okay, I . . . I just have to look after her a lot of the time. That's probably why I haven't been on any climate change marches.' I stop, horrified at myself.

What am I doing?

Earlier, I lied to Gran and Grandad about coming here. And now, I'm telling an awful, terrible lie to Bear and his family.

'How do you fit in your summer job?' Bear asks.

Oh no. I'd forgotten I'd told him I had a job.

'Er, well, that work's just part-time and there are . . . people who pop in to check on Mum . . .' I trail off, desperate to change the subject. 'So . . . do you make things out of the trees in the wood?'

Bear nods. 'We do when we need to. It's all sustainable. Would you like to see the sawmill? It's pretty cool. We don't use any fossil fuels to power it.'

'Yes, please,' I say, feeling relieved at the prospect of getting away from this awkward conversation.

'I'm coming too,' says Skye.

The three of us leave. We wander through the clearing, past a path which Bear explains leads to more homes. I'm vaguely wondering if I'll see Rowan, but the only person we pass is a slim man, about nineteen or twenty, with long, lank hair. He is busy digging up a patch of earth. Beyond him are neat rows of green plants.

'That's the *actual* vegetable garden,' Skye explains.

The man looks up as we go by. He wipes his forehead, gleaming with sweat, and waves. 'Hello there!'

I wave self-consciously back.

'Hello, CJ!' Bear and Skye chorus. 'He's our visitor this month,' Bear explains under his breath. 'Arrived last week.'

As CJ turns back to his spade, his phone rings. It sounds odd, the jingle blasting into the peaceful summer afternoon. Bear, Skye and I walk on.

'Don't you mind not having a phone yourself?' I ask Bear.

He shrugs. 'I'll get one next year. Mum and Drina don't see mobiles the same way most people do. To them, smartphones are like drugs or . . . or gambling; they think it's easy to get addicted. We discussed it and I agreed to wait to have one.'

I'm about to point out how ludicrous this is, then think about Leo spending whole days on his phone. In any case, before I can speak, a loud whirring sound fills the air.

'That's the sawmill,' Skye explains.

We follow the path around a bend and a large, steel machine, positioned under a tarpaulin canopy, comes into view. A huge, circular blade with jagged edges turns round and round, while a white-haired man wearing goggles and gloves pushes a rough plank of wood along some kind of conveyor belt towards it. A woman in a boiler suit, her long hair tied back, is bent over at the other end of the machine, guiding the wood along. They finish cutting the plank as we walk up.

'Hi, guys!' The woman removes her goggles, an easy smile lighting up her face. I like her immediately.

'This is Drina,' Bear says. 'And John.'

John waves, then turns to place the newly cut plank on a stack of others. Drina holds out her hand. I give her mine and she pumps it in a swift, fierce shake. 'And what's your name?' Her brown eyes glint with curiosity.

'Maya,' I say.

Drina casts her eyes quickly over my clothes. I suddenly feel self-conscious. These people might be 'hippies', in the sense that they're living an unconventional life, but not in the fake way that my tiered, boho skirt is. And my top is too white and smart to fit in here.

'Nice to meet you, Maya. Has Bear brought you to see the sawmill?'

I nod. Drina launches into an explanation which I can barely follow. Something about the machine being wood-fired and steam-powered. As soon as she pauses for breath, Bear jumps in.

'We ought to get to the longhouse. I promised I'd show Maya.'

Drina nods, then turns back to her work.

As we walk away, Bear says, 'Sorry about that. Drina loves explaining how everything works.'

I smile at him. 'It's cool.'

Skye skips along beside us. I catch her staring at my little crossbody bag. I can't imagine either her mum or Drina have anything like it.

'Do you ever leave the woods to do ordinary stuff?' I ask.

Bear laughs. 'Of course we do. We go to the shops for the food we can't grow. Not to mention the library and the dentist,' he adds.

'We even went to a Save the Lakes protest up north last month,' Skye adds proudly, shoving her hands into the pockets of her pink shorts.

'Oh.' A chill runs down my spine. Is that the protest Gran mentioned, the one where things got violent?

'It was my first demo,' Skye chatters on. 'It took *ages* to get there. We stopped off on the way and there was a mermaid doll with pink hair at the shop and I really wanted one but Mum and Drina said no.'

Bear rolls his eyes.

I give Skye a sympathetic smile, trying to push my

worries about the protest out of my head. 'Hey,' I say, 'I'm guessing you're really into pink, yes?'

She nods.

I take the lip gloss out of my bag and hand it to her. It's in a pink plastic tube. 'Here, you can have this if you like. It's lip gloss. Bubblegum flavour.'

Skye stops, her eyes wide with delight. 'Really? *Thank you!*'

Bear frowns. 'Um, yeah, thanks, but Skye's too little for make-up.'

'It's really more like lip balm,' I say, feeling embarrassed.

'I *love* it.' Skye hops from foot to foot, an imploring look on her face. 'Please, Bear?'

I grin at her.

Bear shrugs. 'Okay,' he says. 'But don't blame me if Mum takes it away.'

Skye gives me a massive smile, her dimples on show again.

We round a corner and a long, low wooden hut appears in the middle of a clearing. Rows of black solar panels gleam on either side of the building.

'This is the longhouse,' Bear explains. 'It's where we all get together, where all the big decisions are made.'

'Decisions?' I ask. 'About what?'

'Everything to do with the community . . .'

Bear carries on talking, but my attention is taken by the longhouse door, which is slowly opening.

The very last person I want to see steps outside.

NINE

Rowan stands on the longhouse steps, glaring at me.

The smile slides from my face.

'Maya, would you like to come on our local beach clean-up next weekend?' Skye looks up at me, beseeching. 'You said you don't have to look after your mum *all* the time.'

I gaze at Bear, trying to ignore Rowan's scowling face over his shoulder.

Bear nods. 'That would be awesome,' he says. 'If you'd like?'

'Which beach?' I ask.

'Just a couple of miles along the coast,' Bear explains.

'Actually, only proper camp visitors can come with us on official trips.' Rowan strides over. She folds her arms and glares at me. 'And we can't take people wearing sweatshop clothes.'

My throat tightens. I'm not exactly sure what she means, but it's definitely an insult.

'That's ridiculous, Ro,' Bear says.

'Maya can come if she wants,' Skye adds. 'Bear just asked her.'

'That doesn't count,' Rowan snaps.

Anger rises inside me. *What is her problem?* 'D'you mind not talking about me as if I'm not here?' I snap. 'I'd actually really like to help. Isn't *that* what counts?'

Rowan juts out her chin. I'm expecting her to argue, but instead she turns on her heel and stomps off.

Bear tips back his head and roars with laughter as Rowan stalks away. 'That was brilliant,' he says. 'I've never seen Ro lost for words like that.'

I feel triumphant. Okay, so I might have told a couple of lies on the way, but I've only been in Cornwall a day and I already have a job, some new friends *and* I'm getting the better of the local mean girl.

I watch as Rowan turns up a side path.

'Does she live along there?' I ask.

Bear nods, still smiling. 'She's got three little brothers, all younger than Skye, so she has a *lot* of jobs. Puts her in a bad mood most of the time these days. I'm sorry she was rude to you.'

'What did she mean about "sweatshop clothes"?' I gaze down at my skirt, then glance up again at Bear. To my horror, the laughter has completely vanished from his eyes. Instead, he looks mortified, his face the colour of beetroot.

Skye fidgets awkwardly beside him.

'What's the matter?' I ask Bear.

He meets my gaze reluctanly. 'Sweatshop clothes are clothes made really cheaply by people who don't get paid properly,' he explains. 'They're bad for the environment too.'

'Oh, right, yeah. I know about that. I just didn't know that word . . .' I pause. Is Bear embarrassed because he thinks my clothes fall into the 'sweatshop-made' category? He wouldn't be the first person who thought so. Green fashion is a big thing at school and lots of people I know are against cheap clothes, though most of them carry on buying them anyway. It's hard to stop when they're all you can afford and when everyone else has new stuff all the time.

'All our clothes are home-made or second-hand,' Skye adds solemnly. 'And we never buy denim. That's the worst. Making things out of denim uses *gallons* of water.'

'Right, yeah.' I think of the denim shorts I was wearing yesterday when I met Bear and hope he doesn't remember them. 'Of course, that's really bad.'

'It's not only denim,' Bear adds. 'Most manufacturing creates loads of waste water.'

'Really? But . . . but lots of companies these days try to be green, don't they?'

Bear sighs. 'The problem isn't really with individual companies; it's the whole system.'

'Good for profit and politicians. Bad for people and planet,' announces Skye. It sounds like a chant.

We carry on walking. Bear and Skye show me more of the camp, including the dunny and shower Bear mentioned earlier. After a while my phone pings and, when I take it out to check the message, I'm shocked to see it's already almost three o'clock. Gran is texting to remind me to be home for the video call with Mum.

'I'm going to have to go,' I say.

'So will you come to the beach clean-up next week?' Skye asks.

I glance at Bear. He smiles and his eyes crinkle around the edges. My heart gives a funny flip. 'Sure,' I say, trying to keep my voice steady.

We set off through the woods. Bear and Skye leave me at the beach and I hurry back to Gran's, emotions tumbling inside me. I'd bet my entire wardrobe that no one in Bear's family would make violent threats against anyone.

Rude, resentful Rowan, on the other hand . . . that's a different matter entirely. Who knows what she's capable of.

★

66

I get home at quarter past three, still feeling troubled as I let myself in through the back door. Luckily, Gran and Grandad are distracted by the fact that a very grubby Leo has just traipsed a whole load of mud into the house. While Grandad cleans up the mess on the kitchen floor, Gran sends Leo upstairs to put on a clean top before Mum's call.

'Can't have your mother thinking we're letting you walk around in mucky clothes,' Gran says, disappearing up the stairs after him. She calls over her shoulder. 'How was the beach, Maya?'

'Great,' I call back. 'I . . . I met some people.'

'What people?' That's Grandad, poking his head around the kitchen door, his eyes twinkling. 'Surely there isn't a young man in the picture already?'

'Grandad!' I make a face at him. '*Please.*'

Grandad chuckles. I get myself a glass of water from the kitchen while he puts the mop away. As I turn the tap off, I think about Bear and Skye having to fetch their water from the local stream. Not to mention use a communal loo. I can't imagine living like that. A minute later, Gran and Leo reappear. Gran fetches her laptop and props it on the kitchen table. 'Is Harry around?' she asks.

Grandad shakes his head. 'Out till late.'

Gran nods. 'So, Maya . . .' She glances up from her screen. 'Who did you meet earlier?'

I take a deep breath. I can't tell her the truth, not after she told me to avoid the people at the eco camp at all costs. 'Just a boy and a girl about my age, and the boy's little sister,' which is technically true, if lacking in relevant context.

'That's nice,' Gran says. 'Are they locals? Would I know them?'

'Er, I think they might be camping,' I say vaguely. 'Is it okay if I meet up with them next Saturday, on the beach?' I'm being honest here, too. I just haven't said what kind of camping, or which beach.

'Sure.' Gran smiles. 'It's great you're making friends already.'

Encouraged, I sit down at the table beside her. 'The boy I met knows about the environmental group in the wood. He says there's no way they'd be behind the bomb scare at the factory.'

Gran meets my gaze, her eyes suddenly sharp and fierce. 'Well, that's a very naïve position to take,' she says. 'I'm sorry, Maya, but those people are not the harmless hippies they pretend to be. We have proof that they made the hoax bomb call now.'

My head jerks up.

'What proof?'

Gran makes a face. 'It's not enough to arrest them,

unfortunately, but the police have traced the call to a phone box very close to the camp in the woods. We drove past it on our way to the factory yesterday, in fact. We saw some of those eco nutters there too.'

I nod, slowly. An image of Bear's face, scowling at Gran's car, flits through my mind.

'But—'

'The person you saw in the hoodie could easily have been in that group and made the call, then run from the phone box to where you saw them – all in the time frame. It's just like Harry said,' Gran goes on. 'They're extremists who'd do anything to bring down the system.'

As the ringtone for Mum's video call fills the kitchen, I remember Bear's words about the system being the problem and feel more confused than ever.

TEN

I'm preoccupied for the rest of the day. Who is right? Gran and Uncle Harry, certain the Harmony Earth Group are violent revolutionaries? Or Bear, who claims the camp is totally peaceful?

That night, Gran and Grandad insist we play board games – which turns out to be more fun than I'm expecting and at least takes my mind off my worries for a couple of hours. The next day, Sunday, they take me and Leo to a friend's barbecue. There are hardly any kids there, but there is a big swimming pool. It's a sunny day and Leo – much to my surprise – leaves his phone with Gran and takes to the water like he has flippers. He asks me several times to come and swim with him. I take a couple of dips, but mostly I sit out on one of the sun loungers, pretending to read and wondering what Bear is doing right now.

'Please, Maya, the thermometer says the water is 26.5 degrees Celsius,' Leo cries. 'That's the *perfect* tempertaure for the human body.'

I tell him I'm busy and bury my head in my phone.

I haven't forgotten that I said I'd look for shells to use for the Peyton Soaps new product line. Uncle Harry has asked me to show him what I've come up with at work on Monday, and I want to impress him with my research.

I've found loads of pretty shells on the beach, as well as pictures online, but I know Uncle Harry wants something a bit different: something that's youthful and stylish. I scroll through image after image. There's nothing that really grabs me so, in the end, I just select my five favourite shells and save their pictures.

We end up staying at the barbecue until it's dark. On the way back, Leo falls asleep in the car and I have to help Gran get him up the stairs to bed. I go to my own room but I'm not sleepy for ages, my head is too full of shells – and Bear.

Monday morning and I'm trying to decide what to wear for my first day working at Peyton Soaps. After several false starts, I settle on a pair of relatively smart navy joggers and a pale-blue vest top with tiny decorative white buttons down the front. I pin my hair back with a slide and put in my favourite star-shaped earrings for luck. Would Bear say these are sweatshop clothes? They're all from Bonropa or Barata. I realize I have no idea where they were produced or what the conditions were like for the workers who made them. All I know is that they were cheap which, up until now, I've just seen as a good thing.

Gran forces me to eat a slice of wholemeal toast, which I'm too nervous to enjoy, then we get into her car. It's already hot and I wind down my window, letting in a soft, warm breeze. Uncle Harry's Mercedes is still in the drive and the blinds are still drawn at the front window of his garage conversion.

My phone, with all the saved pictures of shells that I think might work for the new product line, is sweaty in my hand.

'Isn't Uncle Harry coming to work today?' I ask.

'Harry makes his own hours. He usually gets in around ten,' Gran explains with an indulgent smile. 'He's very independent.'

We make the short drive to the factory, where Gran hands me over to Parvati. I can tell Gran's already focused on her first meeting from the way she leaves me with a brisk smile and a quick 'Have a good day, Maya'.

Parvati takes me through the empty office area to the much larger, bustling factory floor. It's built in an L shape, with three large machines near the door. The men and women working at them look up as I walk in.

Parvati knows each one by name and stops to introduce me.

'This is Maya, Ms Peyton's granddaughter,' she keeps repeating. 'She's here to help out over the summer.'

Everyone smiles and says, 'Hello,' and 'Welcome!' and I smile back, feeling only a little bit self-conscious. They're all being so friendly.

Past the first set of machines, Parvati leads me over to a big glass-walled room-within-a-room. It's lined with rows and rows of big steel machines sprouting funnels and conveyor belts and giant urn-shaped containers with racks and slides wherever you look. Above the main machine is a gigantic ventilator. Everyone inside the room is wearing blue overalls and proper masks with breathing filters.

'The saponification area,' Parvati explains. 'The heart of what we do. They're just getting ready to make a fresh batch of soap.'

The room is loud with the whirr and clank of metal. Parvati indicates a door in the wall beyond. 'The stockroom,' she explains, 'where we keep all the raw materials.' She takes me over, opening the door so I can see inside. It's a small, square space, with rows of huge plastic canisters lined up on one side and large aluminium cans on the other.

'What's in those?' I ask.

'All the main ingredients for soap-making,' Parvati explains. 'Lye – that's crucial – and distilled water. We mix them, then add vegetable oil and different scents. We—'

'Parvati!' A curt shout makes us both spin around.

A tall man emerges from the small corner office between the stockroom and the fire door. He strides, purposefully, towards us.

'Ah. Hi, there, Artem,' Parvati says, sounding a little nervous. She turns to me. 'This is Artem, the factory manager.' She introduces me quickly.

Artem gives a swift nod in my direction, then points to the stockroom.

'The inventory is not up to date on the computer,' he says, his dark, intense eyes fixed on Parvati's.

'Right, er, sorry, Artem,' she stammers. 'I've just been busy with—'

'It needs to be done,' Artem snaps, then turns on his heel and stalks back to his corner office.

Parvati, her face flushing, closes the stockroom door and ushers me across the factory to the racks of soap at the far end. She's clearly embarrassed by the abrupt way Artem just spoke to her, but she doesn't mention that. Instead, she gabbles away about the company's various products. 'We do soap as solid bars, of course,' she chatters, 'but also as hand wash and shower gel. Then there's the newer hand cream and moisturizer ranges, though we're

74

not manufacturing any of them this week.'

'What about the new Peyton Seashell products?' I ask, thinking of the shell pictures Harry asked me to look at.

'Someone's up to date.' Parvati smiles approvingly. 'No, that range isn't in production yet. How did you know about it?'

'Uncle Harry told me,' I explain.

'Right.' The slightest of shadows passes over Parvati's face at the mention of Harry's name. Before I can think of a way to ask her about him, we arrive at the long racks of fragrant soap. Each shelf is filled with trays of bars, forming an array of colours from sage green to banana yellow and strawberry pink. There's even a row of black soaps. Parvati catches me staring at them.

'Charcoal,' she explains. 'For a detoxifying cleanse.'

I nod, then pick up a soap bar the colour of clotted cream and run my hand over its smooth, waxy surface. A curly $\mathcal{P}$ for 'Peyton' is stamped in the centre, as it is with all the bars. I've seen soaps like this at Gran's house and in shops, of course, but there's something different – and seriously cool – about seeing my own name represented on a bar of soap in the actual place where it's made.

'That one smells of honeysuckle,' Parvati says.

I sniff the bar and a delicate floral aroma fills my nostrils.

'Mmm,' I say. 'That's so nice.'

'Isn't it?' Parvati grins. 'I thought today you might like to work on packaging some of the bars. We hand-wrap everything.' She leads me around the corner into a smaller section of the factory, where two middle-aged women, both called Julie, are folding soap bars into waxy paper, then tying them with strands of raffia.

Parvati leaves and the Julies give me a pair of gloves and show me how to position the bars to get clean corners on the folds. It's repetitive work, but I like it. I quickly get into the rhythm, creasing the wax paper and holding it with my finger while tying the straw-like ribbon. The Julies – who chatter constantly as we work – soon pronounce me 'a professional'. They both have kids a bit older than me and are full of questions about Mum, who they remember from her own holiday jobs at the factory when they were starting out. However, their main topic of conversation is last Friday's bomb scare.

'It were bound to be that load of do-days in the woods,' says the Julie with short blond hair.

'Do-days?' I ask.

'Idiots,' says the Julie with big red-rimmed glasses. 'She means that hippy group living in the woods.'

'The Harmony Earth Group?' I ask.

'Har-*moany* Earth Group, more like,' Blond Julie says

with a chuckle. 'Always complaining about this and that, asking for handouts.'

'Mebbee so,' says Glasses Julie, 'but a bomb scare's a step up from that.'

'There's plenty in that group with criminal records,' Blond Julie says, pursing her lips. 'Nasty, violent people who think that anyone who lives in a nice house is fair game to attack.' She shakes her head. 'It's not right to target your gran. She's a decent boss. Look at the way she paid us double wages on Friday, because of the bomb scare, even though nobody could work.'

'Doesn't she have to pay you?' I ask. 'Legally, I mean?'

'Not double wages, she doesn't,' Glasses Julie says.

'Like I said, she's decent,' Blond Julie adds. 'She cares about the people who work for her. Lots of bosses wouldn't.'

ELEVEN

After a couple of hours, Glasses Julie announces we're overdue a tea break and we troop off to the staffroom. Several of the workers I met earlier on the factory floor sit around two of the three tables. They all smile at me again, though one girl, Hayley, who doesn't look much older than I am, is really sneering more than smiling. She doesn't make eye contact, and leaves the table as soon as the Julies get up to fetch mugs for our tea. I have no idea what her problem is, but I can't be bothered to worry about it. I'm itching to check my phone, so, left alone for a few minutes, I scroll through my social media feeds. They're full of the weekend gossip – who flirted with who, and how they dressed and did their hair, and what happened at Chelsea O'Brien's birthday party on Saturday night. I'd been feeling okay, but the realization that all my friends back in London are carrying on having a great time without me leaves an empty feeling in the pit of my stomach.

The Julies bring me a mug of milky tea then natter away to each other in low voices.

'Morning all!' Uncle Harry cries cheerily from the door.

His presence in the staffroom instantly lightens the atmosphere. Even Hayley grins at him. It's obvious everyone here adores him, just like Gran does. He's probably easier than Gran for the factory staff to get on with, too: friendly and jolly, while she's a bit more stiff and formal.

Uncle Harry chats to the people at one of the other tables for a few minutes, then comes over to where I'm curled up on my chair and says quietly, 'Hey, Maya, shall we talk shells after lunch?'

I nod and he sweeps out. I catch Hayley's eye across the room. The contempt on her face is unmistakable. A few moments later, Blond Julie says it's time to get back to work and we troop back to the factory floor.

I carry on packaging for another hour or so, then Gran fetches me to have lunch in her office. This is a long, narrow room that takes up most of the first floor. It's super quiet, well away from the constant hum of the factory machinery below. A huge desk covered in papers stands opposite rows of box files stacked against the wall. Above the desk, a warm breeze blows in through the open skylight set into the slanted roof.

I wander over to the other window, at the far end of

the room. It looks out over a sheer drop to the ground beneath. A moment later Uncle Harry joins us, with sandwiches for him and me and a salad for Gran. He puts the food down, then clears a stack of paper off the chair in the corner so he can sit down.

'We have your grandad to thank for our lunch,' Gran says proudly to me. 'He likes to make sure I get a healthy meal, even when I'm busy.'

I clear another chair for myself and unwrap my sandwiches. They're chicken and salad on what I know is Grandad's home-made wholemeal bread, with the tomatoes and cucumbers all cut up into tiny pieces. They taste delicious. As I lift the second sandwich off its wrapper, I spot a little note Grandad has left for me:

Have a great first day! Remember, every journey begins with a single step!

I show Gran.

Uncle Harry grins. 'Did you get one of Dad's motivational messages?' and I nod.

'He's reminding Maya she's at the start of a brand-new adventure,' Gran says with a smile. 'It makes perfect sense.'

'Sure,' I say.

'Tell you what *doesn't* make sense,' Uncle Harry says,

his eyes twinkling at Gran – 'your filing system. All this paper. What a mess!'

'Everything's on the computer as well,' Gran retorts. 'I just like paper copies. I miss things when I read onscreen.'

I munch hungrily away as Uncle Harry meets my gaze. He rolls his eyes and I suppress a giggle.

'When *I'm* in charge,' he says, 'I'm going to clear all the old files out of this room. Make it a totally paper-free workplace.'

Gran tuts. 'I've still got a few years in me yet, you know.' The two of them grin at each other. What a massive difference there is between the jokey, easy way Gran gets on with her son and the more awkward relationship she has with Mum.

After we've eaten, Uncle Harry takes me back downstairs to the open-plan office and asks to see the shell pictures I've selected. I'm a bit nervous before we start – the more shells I looked at, the less I thought they were really the right visual image for something aimed at teenagers – but Uncle Harry is really complimentary about everything I've picked.

'These are great choices,' he says. 'I'm going to put them all on the mood board for the agency.'

'Thanks, but . . .' I hesitate, not sure if my querying Uncle Harry's idea will sound rude.

'What?' he asks. 'Go on.'

'It's just . . .' I wrinkle my nose. 'I'm not sure if shells aren't . . . well, aren't they a bit old-fashioned, maybe?'

Uncle Harry frowns. 'What, you're suggesting we . . . we rethink the entire brand? The whole Peyton Seashell range?' He doesn't sound angry. Just confused.

I nod, slowly.

Uncle Harry blows out his breath. 'Well,' he says, 'I guess we *could* . . . We're still in the early stages. None of the new soaps are actually in production yet. But . . . but what would we use as our new concept? It needs to be something outdoorsy that fits with our overall image, but . . . well, I just can't think what might fit the bill . . .' He trails off.

'What about rainbows?' I ask, sitting up. 'The Peyton Rainbow range? It's still outdoors-sounding, but much younger than seashells. Plus rainbows are—'

'Inclusive!' Uncle Harry's eyes widen. 'That's a great idea.'

I grin. 'Really?'

'Definitely. I'm going to brief the brand agency tomorrow, get them thinking about ways to use your rainbow concept to create a funky and youthful vibe.'

'Will you let me know what they say?'

'Course I will,' Uncle Harry says. 'And I'll also make

sure they know we have a budding brand designer on the premises who came up with a better idea for our new range than all of them put together!'

I sit back, blushing and feeling very pleased with myself.

Three p.m. arrives faster than I'd have imagined. The factory workers don't leave until four, but Gran says she quite often works at home during the later part of the afternoon and that I'm to go home with her. We leave Uncle Harry preparing the brief for his meeting with the design company tomorrow and we drive home.

'So, how did you enjoy your first day?' Gran asks, as we turn onto the main road.

'I loved it,' I say. And I mean it.

The rest of the week passes in a similar way. Grandad makes a packed lunch for me and Gran every day, which we eat together in Gran's office. Most days he puts a note in for me too. Random stuff like:

Just when the caterpillar thought the world was ending, he turned into a butterfly.

And:

You will never win if you never begin.

My favourite so far is:

It isn't the climb that wears you out, it's the pebble in your shoe.

Uncle Harry doesn't join me and Gran for lunch again but he makes sure to ask how I am every day, and I notice that wherever he goes in the factory, people smile.

After work most days, Gran takes me and Leo onto the secluded strip of beach in front of the house. The weather stays warm and, while Gran sits under an umbrella reading work reports, Leo makes intricate sandcastles, carefully consulting Grandad's dog-eared *Illustrated History of Forts and Castles* as he goes.

Meanwhile, I search my phone, scanning the new Bonropa outfits I'm planning to buy with my first pay packet. Occasionally, people Gran knows pass by and stop for a quick chat. Even though this is a fairly deserted bit of sand, and at least a twenty-minute walk from the edge of the wood where I met with Bear, I'm still worried in case someone from the Harmony Earth Group sees me here, with Gran. I keep my eyes open, but thankfully nobody from the camp appears.

84

★

Saturday comes around soon and, with it, my visit to the beach clean-up with Bear. I choose my clothes carefully, making sure to avoid wearing any denim. Finally, dressed in plain black joggers and a grey sweatshirt, I add a slick of mascara, tell Gran I'm meeting up with my new friends for a day on the beach, and set off to meet Bear.

I start to feel a bit jittery as I get close to the edge of the wood. What's it going to be like when I see him? Will he have thought twice and not bothered to come? And what if he's there but I can't think of anything to say?

I needn't have worried. Bear's waiting for me, a big smile on his face. He launches straight into a question, asking how far I've had to walk to get here. Immediately I make up a story about living on the outskirts of Penwillick. I don't like telling the lie, but at least it leaves no time for me to feel nervous about being with him.

Soon we're chatting away like old friends. Today he's dressed in cotton trousers with the bottoms rolled up, and a long-sleeved top, both of which make him look older than he did before. His hair is different too – tied neatly back off his face into a tiny ponytail. I can't decide if he's looking more grown-up by accident, or whether he's made a special effort. If he has, is it for my benefit? The thought makes me smile to myself.

The sea is at low tide and we walk together along the shore, in and out of a series of small bays for what seems like miles. Apart from a sprinkling of families sunbathing on towels and splashing in the shallows, they are mostly clean and empty.

'These beaches don't look like they need cleaning up,' I point out.

Bear makes a face. 'Just wait till we get to Litterbug Cove. The tide washes loads of stuff up there – it's terrible.' He shakes his head.

We walk along the damp sand, close to the water. It's almost a cliché how romantic it is, with the sun shining and the sea sparkling and the two of us kicking off our shoes to feel the splash of the gentle waves on our feet. Even so, everything I've heard about the eco group keeps running through my head. It's not just Gran and Uncle Harry who think the Harmony Earth Group are dangerous. Didn't Blond Julie say that it was full of violent criminals? And she's clearly not the only one at the factory who doesn't like them.

Can so many people be wrong?

'Is something on your mind?' Bear asks, lightly.

I take a deep breath. 'Somebody . . . er, told me that people from your camp got arrested after a protest up north turned into a fight? I remembered you and Skye mentioning a protest like that the other day. Was that the one?'

'Yes, but it wasn't anyone from *our* camp in the fight. And nobody from Harmony Earth Group was arrested.' Bear sighs. 'We'd left by then.'

'So why do people think your group was involved?' I ask, genuinely baffled.

'Because it's what they *want* to think,' Bear says bitterly. 'They're prejudiced against us because we live in a different way. Mum says they feel threatened, but it's not fair. We get the blame for everything.' He glances at me. 'Like that bomb scare last week at Peyton Soaps.'

'Oh?' I meet his gaze, hoping he won't see how awkward I feel.

'Yeah. The police spoke to Drina, asking loads of questions about everyone living at the camp.'

'Really?'

'Apparently someone saw a "hooded figure" running from the factory towards our wood.'

My stomach churns. 'Who . . . er . . . do you know who said that?'

Bear shrugs. 'Someone who works at Peyton, I think.'

'I see.'

'Whoever it was is probably as prejudiced against us as

the owner.' Bear rolls his eyes. 'It also turns out that the phone call saying there was a bomb came from a phone box near our camp. As if either of those things prove anything. In fact, surely it's obvious that if someone at our camp wanted to make a call like that they'd go further away?'

I nod in agreement.

'But a bomb scare . . .' he says, 'that's serious. That's *terrorism*.'

He's right. I can't imagine anyone at his camp going that far.

'Here we are,' Bear says, as we round a high cliff and walk into the next bay.

I gasp. Rubbish covers the sand, all the way up to the rock face. In places it's knee high: aluminium cans, broken cardboard boxes and ripped plastic bags are scattered across tyres and bits of metal. There's even half a rusty old bike lying on its side. And, across it all, an endless spread of plastic bags and bottles in all shapes and sizes.

'Welcome to Litterbug Cove,' Bear says grimly.

A group of about twelve people, all wearing tough gardening gloves, are spread out, gathering up the rubbish into large sacks. I spot Bear's mum and Drina straight away, examining a long, empty blister pack of pills. Skye stands beside them, shoving metal bottle caps into a bag.

Her red hair is tied into a ponytail finished with a hot-pink ribbon. She sees us and waves enthusiastically. Bear and I walk over, past John, the white-haired man from the sawmill, who is carefully detangling a clump of plastic cables. Further along the beach, Rowan is part of a bigger group picking up a broken office chair.

'How many of the camp are here?' I ask.

'Most of the adults,' Bear says. 'None of the little kids, except Skye. She's only here because she's good at sticking close to Mum and Drina. It's dangerous, you see – there could be something sharp or even toxic.'

The sea blows its salty breeze over our faces as we cross the beach. 'How come all this rubbish ends up here, in this one place?'

'Something to do with the the tides, I think.' Bear frowns. 'Bad isn't it?'

I nod.

'Hello, Maya,' Bear's mum says as we approach. 'Nice to see you again.'

'It's really great you came to help,' Skye adds, beaming.

'Yes, it's very much appreciated,' says Drina. She hands me a pair of thick, padded gloves and a hessian sack. 'Here you are. Be careful what you touch: there are some things here with sharp edges.'

'And call us over immediately if it's liquid or marked

"toxic" or "poison",' Bear's mum adds.

I stare at her alarmed.

'Don't worry, we've already done an initial check,' Drina says. 'We're just being super cautious.'

I nod. 'How long is it since you were last here?'

'About three months,' Bear's mum says.

My eyes widen. 'This much rubbish in just three months!'

'And this is just the tip of the iceberg,' Drina says, sourly. 'There're also the pesticides and chemicals and untreated sewage we can't see polluting the water.'

'And harming all the living things *in* it,' Bear adds miserably.

'Can't somebody stop this happening?' I ask. 'Or at least clean up the beach so you don't have to?'

Drina gives a dry laugh. 'I wish,' she says. 'But the police appear to be more interested in barging into our camp and harassing us about a local bomb scare.'

'Oh,' I say, feeling awkward again. 'Yeah, Bear mentioned something about that.'

Drina rolls her eyes. 'Honestly, people take one look at us and start jumping to conclusions.'

I shuffle uncomfortably from side to side.

Bear tugs me away. 'Come on, let's get started.'

I follow him across the beach and put on the gloves

Drina gave me. Bear and I work silently, examining the rubbish and putting what we can into our bags. I'm aware as we make our way along the sand that we're getting closer to Rowan. She's already glanced up a few times and given me evils. Bear doesn't seem to have noticed. Another few minutes finds us alongside her.

'Hi, Maya,' Rowan says brightly. To my surprise she's now smiling at me.

'Hi,' I say, warily.

'How are you?' Rowan asks. 'And how is your poor mum?' She makes a sympathetic face.

'Okay, thanks.' I can feel my face flushing. Trust Rowan to hone right in on that stupid lie I told about my mum being ill.

I hesitate, my throat dry. Rowan stands there, hands on her hips, still smiling. She's wearing shorts and a blue tunic top that totally brings out the colour of her eyes. With her tanned skin and tousled hair, she looks like a model just finished with a beach shoot.

'What exactly is wrong with your mum?' Rowan asks, the same even, kindly tone in her voice. 'You said you have to look after her all week.' She pauses. 'Is she, like, in a wheelchair or something?'

I'm sure my face is bright red now. I glance at Bear. Thankfully, he's not paying us any attention. He's bent over a grubby collection of plastic bottles, scooping them into his bag. The sun emerges from behind a white fluffy cloud.

'No, she's not in a wheelchair,' I say hesitantly, shielding my eyes from the sudden glare. 'She's just got a condition which, um, it . . . it makes her tired.' I'm trying to sound specific enough to be convincing and vague enough that Rowan won't pin me down to a particular illness or disease.

'Right.' Rowan stops smiling. A seagull squawks overhead. 'And this "condition" means you have to stay indoors with her all the time?' She's still smiling sympathetically, but there's a new, sceptical note to her voice. Bear, who must have been listening after all, looks up.

'I don't have to stay with Mum *all* the time,' I say quickly. 'It's just . . . just not easy to get away. I have to make sure someone's there, looking out for her.'

'Oh, really?' Rowan says, now openly sneering. 'Is that so?'

Bear lets his rubbish bag fall to the sand with a thud. 'What is your problem, Ro?'

'It's not *me* that has the problem,' Rowan counters. 'It's Maya.'

'What's that supposed to mean?' I demand.

'I'm just wondering,' Rowan says smoothly, 'how you manage to deal with the problem of needing to be in two places at once.'

'*What?*' Bear and I speak together.

A mean smile creeps across Rowan's lips. 'You know,' she says. 'Being at home with your mum *and*, at the same time, doing your job at Peyton Soaps.'

TWELVE

I stare at Rowan. My heart is beating so loudly I'm certain she and Bear will hear it.

'Maya doesn't work at Peyton Soaps,' Bear says indignantly, then turns to me and, less confidently, asks: 'do you?'

Rowan glares at me, her bright blue eyes so intense it's like she can see right through me.

I think fast.

'It's complicated,' I say. 'My mum used to work at the factory years ago. When we came back last month the boss, Ms Peyton, gave me a summer job to help out. She's been really nice about Mum being ill. The job's just a few hours a day, hand-wrapping soaps and . . . and that sort of thing.' I stop, feeling slightly breathless.

'I thought you said you couldn't leave your mum?' Rowan asks, her lips curling in a sneer.

'For goodness' sake, Ro,' Bear snaps. 'Maya told us about her summer job the first time we met.'

'That's right,' I say quickly. 'Our neighbour pops in

to check on Mum while I'm at work.' I stop again, part thrilled, part appalled by the ease with which the lies are tumbling out of me.

'Do you think your mum might have been made ill by the chemicals they use at Peyton Soaps?' Bear asks.

'No,' I say, then worried that I sounded too emphatic, add: 'At least, I don't *think* so.'

Bear and Rowan exchange a look. Bear shakes his head. 'Drina says with conditions like your mum's, with her being exhausted all the time, that sometimes they can be down to exposure to toxins.' His clear, pale-green eyes are full of such genuine concern. Inside I'm squirming with guilt.

'I really don't think Mum being ill has anything to do with Peyton Soaps,' I say, unable to meet his gaze. 'Ms Peyton is always saying how green they are there.'

'Right.' Rowan gives a sceptical sniff. 'Maybe she doesn't want you to realize how *toxic* they are.' She narrows her eyes. 'Perhaps that's why she gives you lifts in her car, to try and buy your silence.'

How does Rowan know I travel to and from work with Gran? How, in fact, does she know I'm working at the factory at all?

'Have you been spying on me?' I demand.

'Yeah.' Bear frowns. 'How come you're up on all this, Ro?'

'I saw you on Monday in that old lady boss's car. The window was down and you were wearing a blue top and star-shaped earings.' Rowan stares at me, an unmistakable look of triumph in her eyes.

'Ms Peyton gives me a lift because Mum and I live on her way home,' I say. It's not hard to sound indignant, even though I'm lying.

'I think you owe Maya an apology, Rowan,' Bear says curtly. 'She's working to help look after her mum and she never lied about *anything*.'

I fix my focus on my canvas pumps.

Rowan blinks, clearly shocked. 'You aren't angry that she didn't mention working at Peyton Soaps?'

'Of course not!' Bear snaps. 'Now why don't you get on with your own rubbish-picking and leave us alone?'

I gasp. Rowan presses her lips together, hesitating for a second, then she turns and stalks away, her hessian sack dangling from her hand.

'I'm really sorry she was so rude,' Bear says. 'I don't know what's got into her recently.'

She likes you, I think.

Then, immediately, *I* like you.

Do you like me?

My cheeks burn at this thought. 'Thanks,' I say, trying to swallow down my embarrassment.

'I just . . .' Bear hesitates. 'I don't understand. Why didn't you mention you worked at Peyton Soaps when we were talking about the bomb scare earlier?'

I shrug, the heat in my face now spreading through my entire body. 'Oh, look –' I point to a cluster of cans on their side on the sand – 'Is that just paint? Or something more dangerous?'

Bear bends down, examining the nearest can. 'Just paint,' he says.

We pick up the cans in silence, then move on to a scattering of ripped plastic bags. A soft breeze wafts towards us, the salt of the sea scenting the air. If it wasn't for the rubbish all around us and the knot of anxiety in my stomach, it would be kind of idyllic.

'So what's it like, working at Peyton's?' Bear asks.

'It's okay,' I say, suddenly feeling guilty for not sticking up more strongly for the company earlier. 'They've got all these green policies and I think the boss, Ms Peyton, she's genuinely trying to be environmentally friendly. She says they treat their waste water and recycle all their rubbish . . .' I hesitate. 'Anyway, soap is clean – it can't be *that* bad for the environment.'

Bear laughs. 'You wouldn't believe what some companies try and get away with.'

'Like what?' I ask.

'There's one which keeps dumping its packaging along a track just off the main road into Polborne.'

'What . . . just leaving the rubbish there?'

'Yup. They dump the waste and it rolls down the hill by the track and into a stream. That's how we found out. Mum was monitoring water purity in the area. She followed the stream we use for fresh water and found the rubbish and traces of various chemicals. We told the council and the water board, but apparently the contamination wasn't bad enough so they did nothing.' He sighs. 'Anyway, we're monitoring it ourselves now.'

'How d'you know it's just one company?'

'It's always the same pattern. They take the labels off the containers, so we can't trace them back to where they're from. Which means there isn't much for the police to go on. Not that the police would probably do anything. Mum says they don't see waste dumping as a big priority.'

'Right,' I say.

'Anyway,' Bear goes on, 'we set up a camera, and a van brings a new load soon after midnight, on the first Thursday of the month. At least, that's what they did in June and July.' He makes a face. 'Unfortunately, both times the van had its lights dipped and our camera was too far away to make out anything useful like the registration plate.'

I stare at him. 'The first Thursday of August is this week.'

Bear nods. 'And this time Mum and Drina say I can go with them. We just need some proper info to take to the police. Or, if they won't help, so we can try and trace the van back to its owner and expose them on socical media.'

'That's so cool.' My chest tightens with excitement. 'Could . . . could I come with you?'

'Sure,' Bear says, looking pleased.

We go over to Bear's mum and Drina to check they don't mind me joining the group on Thursday.

'We'd love to have you with us,' Bear's mum says with a smile, 'so long as your mother doesn't object.'

'Oh, she won't,' I say, confidently. 'Mum is really into protecting the environment.' This isn't strictly true, but as a lie it doesn't seem any worse than the ones I've told so far. It will mean sneaking out of the house, of course. Gran is fairly easy about me going out during the day, but I can't imagine she'd be happy for me to take part in a night-time spying operation with people she thinks are violent criminals.

As Bear and I walk down to the shore, Skye skips over. She's holding my lip gloss tube in one hand and a small, round stone in the other. 'Hey, Maya!' She sounds excited. 'I just found *such* a pretty pebble!'

I take the little stone she's offering. It *is* pretty: perfectly round and smooth, with a swirl of pearly pink, like a wave, across the middle.

'That's beautiful,' I say, smiling. Skye's eyes light up. 'You should take it home,' I say, handing the stone back to her.

She looks at me, shocked. 'No *way!*' she says. 'Pebbles belong on the beach.'

'Right,' I say, feeling embarrassed. 'Of course.'

The three of us take a break from the rubbish-collecting and sit on the sand, dabbling our feet in the water and eating the soft, sweet rolls Bear's mum has brought for everyone. I can't see Rowan anywhere. Much to my relief, it looks like she's left already. Bear explains where and when we should meet on Thursday, while Skye huddles close to me, even resting her head against my arm at one point.

'She's usually really shy with strangers,' Bear says as Skye skips off back to her mum and Drina. 'I think she likes the idea of having an older sister.'

'I like the idea of having a younger one,' I say. 'I only have a little brother, Leo. He's great, but I've always thought a sister would be nice too.'

'Sometimes,' Bear says with a grin.

I smile back. It's a relief to say something true and uncomplicated for once.

★

That evening, after another video call with Mum, everyone at home – even Uncle Harry – sits down at the kitchen table for dinner. Leo gets noticeably miserable, his shoulders slumped over his bowl. He must miss Mum a lot. I do too, of course, but my head's so full work and Bear that I probably don't think about her as much as he does.

Gran and Grandad exchange a worried look.

'How about another round of Go?' Gran asks, briskly.

Leo shakes his head.

'Or we could wait until it's dark and go out to the astronomy hut?' Grandad suggests, patting Leo's hand. 'It's a bit cloudy, but you never know.'

Leo does look up at this, but only to say: 'Thank you, but it mightn't be fun if we can't see much', before sinking back into his chair again.

I stare at him, feeling anxious.

'I know what we'll do,' Uncle Harry says cheerily. 'You guys are coming over to my place tonight. I'm going to teach you how to play Bumper Bonanza.'

I make a face. 'What's that?'

'You'll see!' Harry looks at Leo. 'You up for that?'

Leo nods, a faint glimmer of interest in his eyes.

I don't really want to play Uncle Harry's game, but it's nice that he's trying to cheer up Leo. I guiltily realize how little attention I've given my little brother recently. He's had to cope with a lot since we arrived: not just missing Mum, but getting used to a whole new routine with Gran and Grandad as well.

After dinner, the three of us walk through the connecting door in the utility room and into Uncle Harry's flat. It's cosy, with an open-plan living area where the garage once was and a bedroom and shower room built on at the far end. The place is much messier than Gran's house: the floor is scattered with clothes and shoes and empty pizza boxes, while the small countertop at the kitchenette end of the living area is submerged under plates and bowls, the largest of which contains a big bunch of keys. Leo makes straight for the leather sofa, which is positioned in front of the biggest TV I've ever seen. He sits down in the middle, then looks up expectantly.

'Is Bumper Bonanza a video game?' he asks.

Uncle Harry nods and my heart sinks. I've never been into those.

'It's like bumper cars, but you win points and prizes as you work through the levels. You're both going to love it.'

Funnily enough, he's right. We end up having a great evening. Uncle Harry is kind and patient as he explains the game – and really good fun when we play it. Thankfully, Leo cheers up completely. He's his normal, enthusiastic self the next day too when Gran and Grandad take us to an old castle. He drags us through the ruins, gabbling away about how each area would have been used hundreds of years ago, until Gran declares that she's exhausted and insists we all sit down for a picnic.

It's fun seeing Leo so excited. I'm excited too – but not about the ancient castle. All I can think about is the eco group's spying mission coming up on Thursday.

Of course, there's the early part of the week to get through first. I spend most of it with the packaging Julies – and discussing the new Peyton Rainbow range with Uncle Harry. He asks me what I think about a range of patterns and colours – which ones seem youthful and relevant and which seem old-fashioned and boring – before he heads off to another meeting with the branding agency. He takes everything I say super seriously, even making notes when I talk!

On Wednesday I do some filing for Parvati, then it's back to wrapping soaps, though Gran also gets the factory manager, Artem, to show me how a soap bar is created from start to finish. It's weird. I'd never have thought I'd be interested in anything to do with factory machinery, but it's cool seeing something being made out of nothing.

Especially when the initial letter of your very own surname gets embossed onto it at the end.

By the time Thursday arrives, I'm totally used to my new life in Penwillick. I've hardly looked at my social media for the past few days. All the fun stuff at home in London that I'm missing – and that used to seem so important – has faded away. I like how different I feel here, treated like a grown-up *and* earning money along the way. Grandad's lunchtime note sums it all up exactly:

There is only one time that is important: now!

Gran is out at a meeting so I'm eating alone in her office. I've just finished my sandwiches when Uncle Harry bounds into the room.

'I wanted to let you know what I've decided to do with the new range,' he exclaims.

'Ooh, what?' I sit up, wiping my mouth.

'The products are all fragrance-free, so the branding is crucial. I talked through the shapes and colours you picked with the guys at the agency,' Uncle Harry goes on, settling himself into the chair opposite Gran's desk, 'and the main designer was really impressed, says you've got a great eye and that you should really think about going into brand design.'

'Seriously?' I swell with pride.

'That's not all,' Uncle Harry says, clasping his hands behind his head and leaning back. 'We decided to go with dynamic, abstract images on the packaging and to give the various products youthful names, all of which are associated with the sea – in keeping with our overall brand.'

'Names associated with the sea?' I ask.

Uncle Harry nods. 'Water-inspired names like Mizuko, Dalila and Sarila and . . .' He pauses, sitting forward and fixing my gaze. 'And Maya.'

I stare at him. 'Maya?' My eyes widen. 'Do you mean it?'

'Yes!' He grins. 'Maya means "water" in . . .' He frowns. 'Er, I can't remember which language. The important thing is: it's settled. We have the soap almost ready to go – a strong, vibrant blue bar, designed for sensitive skins – and it'll be named after you!' He pauses. 'What do you think?'

'I think it's amazing,' I say, unable to stop smiling. My own name on a range of soaps, imagine! 'That's even better than the embossed P for Peyton. Thank you!'

'Thank *you*,' Uncle Harry says. 'If it wasn't for your input, we'd still be faffing about with seashells.'

★

My nerves start building once I'm back at home for the evening. I go up early, then sit in my room waiting for everyone else to go to bed. I'm due to meet Bear at the junction of Penwillick Wood and Polborne Road at midnight. I hear Gran and Grandad switching out the lights just after eleven, then silence. I check my trainers are tied tight and that my phone is on vibrate only and in my pocket. I'm wearing black leggings and a long, dark jacket. Bear didn't say anything about how to dress, but I don't need to be told that spying missions require clothes that won't stand out from the shadows.

After half an hour or so. I check my phone again. Time to go.

THIRTEEN

I creep out of my bedroom and stand on the landing, listening for signs that anyone else is still awake. The house is completely silent. The nightlight outside Leo's bedroom creates a soft, blue glow along the carpet, towards the stairs. I step carefully over the creaky top step, then pad down to the ground floor. My palms are sweaty as I slide the bolts then open the front door and slip outside. Even though I'm being super careful, the door closes behind me with a loud click. I freeze, straining to catch any movement inside. Gran and Grandad's bedroom is only a few metres away . . . I hear nothing.

Relieved, I hurry across the drive and along the private road. The night air is cool, full of the salty smell of the sea and so quiet that even from here I catch the soft slap and swish of the distant waves. These sounds fade as I turn onto the main road. Keeping close to the hedge, I pull the hood of my jacket over my head and hurry towards my meeting place with Bear. There's no traffic about and no street lamps, but the soft, ivory, almost-full moon casts a path of light ahead of me. I stay on the grassy verge beside the road, feeling more than a little spooked by the silence and the darkness. The high hedges either side cast weird shadows all around me. An owl hoots, making me jump. Then two cars whizz past, fast, one after the other. The whoosh of their engines echoes in my ears.

In fifteen minutes I reach the junction of Penwillick Wood and Polborne Road. Where is Bear? For a brief, horrible moment I think he's forgotten me.

'I wasn't sure you'd actually turn up,' he says softly, stepping out from behind a tree.

Moonlight glints off his streaked-blond hair, sparkling in his eyes and highlighting his cheekbones.

'Ah, well, I did,' I say. Which isn't exactly inspired, but the best I can do with the way my heart is now thudding.

'I'm glad.' Bear holds out his hand. I take it, feeling a thrill of electricity pass through me as his warm fingers press against mine. 'Come on, the others are waiting for us,' he says. 'It's about a ten-minute walk from here.'

Bear keeps hold of my hand as we walk along the verge beside the Polborne Road. Above us, the dark sky is sprinkled with thousands of tiny stars.

'Wow,' I say, looking up. 'There are so *many*.'

Bear laughs, his eyes crinkling.

We walk on. A few cars zoom noisily by, then disappear

into darkness. After a while, we turn left off the main road. Bear lets go of my hand and leads me along an unmarked track. Trees rise up on the right, and soon we can no longer see the road we've just turned off. To our left is a short, steep hillside, dotted with trees and bushes. The path leads down to a shallow stream, whose water gleams in the moonlight.

'Is this where the dumping happens?' I ask, my voice low.

Bear nods. 'Somewhere along here. There's about a hundred metres just like this. There's no way we can tell exactly where they're going to tip their rubbish.'

I look around. The track continues ahead of us, for as far as I can see. There's no sign of another person. 'Where is everyone?' I ask.

Bear points down the hill, where two figures are emerging from behind a large, thick bush: Drina and Bear's mum, Val. We say hello and Drina directs us about fifty metres further along the track.

'There's a big oak tree about halfway down the hillside,' she says. 'You can't miss it. Hide behind that.'

'How many other people are here?' I ask.

'Eight altogether,' Bear's mum explains. 'We're spread out, taking cover wherever we can. Hopefully *one* of us will get a good look at the van.'

'And the driver,' Drina adds. 'Any information that can help us track down who's behind the waste dumping will be good.'

Bear and I nod, then hurry on.

We find the oak tree easily enough. It's huge, offering plenty of cover as we crouch down behind it. A gust of wind brushes, cold, across my face. I shiver, tugging my jacket more tightly around me, then check the time on my phone: I've been out longer than I thought. It's almost half past midnight.

'When d'you think the van will come?' I whisper.

Bear shrugs. 'Could be two minutes or two hours, it depends on—'

'I thought it was you.' Rowan appears out of the darkness. CJ, the camp visitor I saw working on the vegetable patch on my first visit, is at her side. 'Hi, Maya, how are you? It's so awesome that you're here.'

'I'm good, thanks,' I say, feeling unsettled. How come she's being so polite? Rowan is still smiling at me, clearly expecting more of a response. 'It's cool, being here . . .' I stammer. 'Being part of this.'

Rowan nods. 'I know, right? Although –' she makes a face – 'if it were up to me, we'd stop the van driver *before* he dumped his disgusting rubbish.'

'And make him pay for dumping it,' CJ adds with a snarl.

'How would you do that?' I stare at them. Are they hinting that they might use violence? 'How far would you go?'

Rowan frowns.

'I'd do whatever it takes,' CJ says. 'It's not right these dumpers get away with it.'

'That's exactly why we don't try and stop them,' Bear says, with a wry chuckle. 'We don't know how they'd react if we challenged them. Someone could get hurt. We're just here to get info on the van – and the driver – that we can take to the authorities or expose on social media.'

'Yeah, your mum's already made that point.' CJ gives a disparaging sniff.

'I just hate that we have to let them get away with it,' Rowan grumbles.

Bear rolls his eyes. I'm guessing it isn't the first time they've argued about this and I relax a little. Surely this proves, once and for all, that even if some members of the camp would like to go further, violence really isn't part of the group's agenda.

'At least we clear up their mess,' Bear points out. 'That's *something*, isn't it?'

'I guess,' Rowan says with a sigh. 'It's still—'

'Sssh!' I interrupt, as the rumble of an engine sounds in the distance. 'Can you hear that?'

The four of us crouch low to the ground as two bright headlights appear along the track. I shrink against the oak tree, my heart thumping. Bear's hand presses lightly on my arm.

'Rowan, let's go back to where your dad's hiding,' CJ breathes. 'He reckons that's where the van's most likely to stop.'

'Wait—' Bear starts, but Rowan and CJ have already vanished into the darkness.

I gaze at the vehicle along the track. I can just make out its shape now. As it trundles towards us, the headlamps dip, bouncing along the uneven ground in front of it.

'That van isn't slowing down where Ro's dad thought it would,' Bear whispers.

'No,' I say, a thrill snaking down my spine. 'It's making straight for *us*.'

Seconds tick away as the van comes closer and closer. I hold my breath as it pulls up on the track, just a few metres above where we're hiding. I peer around the tree. It's impossible from here to make out the registration number. I can't even tell what colour the van is. Black, maybe, or dark blue?

The thud of a door indicates the driver is getting out. Seconds later he appears: stockily built, wearing gloves and a cap pulled low on his forehead. I can't see his face.

He opens the van's back doors and starts hauling out a series of metal containers, sending them hurtling down the hillside towards the stream at the bottom.

'Damn,' Bear whispers, his breath hot against my ear. 'We're too far away to see anything useful.'

The driver has already chucked out what must be half the contents of the van. Strips of dented metal, flattened cardboard packaging and bundles of stiff plastic sheeting follow the containers down the hill. A series of big plastic bottles, like the ones used for storing distilled water at the factory, bump past the tree. If I could just get a little way up the hillside, I could use my phone to take a picture, not just of the van, but of the driver himself.

'I'm going to get a bit closer,' I whisper.

'No, it's too danger—' Bear reaches out to grab my arm but I dart away.

I stay in the shadows, crouching low as I run up to the front of the van, then creep silently alongside it. The thumps of the last few bottles and containers hitting the ground echo towards me. I can see the van driver more clearly now: he's pushed his cap back off his forehead and the thick, dark lines of his eyebrows stand out against his pale face. Sweat gleams on his brow as he hauls a huge plastic barrel out of the back of the van and rolls it across the grass.

I take out my phone, careful to shield its light with my body, and check that the camera flash is switched off and I'm in video mode. Eyebrows man moves, blocking my view of the barrel he's dumping. I take a tiny step forward, trying to get a better angle. My foot knocks against the turned-out wheel. I stumble, thrown off balance—

'Aagh!' A yelp flies out of my mouth.

I freeze, terror coursing through me.

Eyebrows' head jerks up. He stops heaving stuff out of the van. I shrink against the side of the van, fear shooting like ice up my spine.

Eyebrows grunts. 'What the . . . ?' he mutters.

I press my cheek against the van's cold metal. The dry earth crunches as Eyebrows takes a step in my direction.

Another second and he'll see me.

FOURTEEN

I sink down and slip, silently, under the van. I lie flat against the damp earth as Eyebrows' trainers appear, just an arm's length away from me. He paces up and down, the frayed ends of his jeans trailing in the dirt. He stops by the van's front left wheel. The hubcap is broken, leaving a jagged edge through which I watch him turn around, clearly peering into the trees beyond.

Another hoarse yelp, very similar to mine but pitched slightly lower echoes across the night air. It's coming from the tree where I left Bear. Two more yelps follow, in quick succession.

Eyebrows shakes his head. 'Foxes,' he murmurs to himself.

He strides past me again, then disappears around the corner of the van. As another canister thuds to the ground, I wriggle out from under the vehicle, glance over my shoulder to make sure Eyebrows isn't watching me, then stand up. I'm shaking all over. Keeping low, I hurry away from the van, into the shadows. As I loop around, heading back to our tree, the van doors slam shut and the engine revs.

Bear stands as I approach. He stares at me, mouth gaping. Over his shoulder I can see the van disappearing along the gloomy track.

'Are you okay?' he gasps.

I nod, shivering. He pulls me towards him and hugs me. The warmth of his body filters through my jacket.

'That was you, right? Making the fox noise?' I ask, drawing back.

'Sure was.' Bear's eyes twinkle in the soft glow of the moonlight. 'That was *mad* what you did,' he says. 'I was terrified that guy was going to see you. Did you get a picture?'

I make a face. 'No, I—'

'Hey, guys, what happened?' Drina and Bear's mum are hurrying towards us. Behind them other people, including Rowan and a man with the same wild curls as her – he must be her dad – emerge from the shadows. I spot CJ again, and white-haired John, the retired solicitor.

Everyone stares at us.

Bear quickly explains that we couldn't get a clear view of the van's number plate.

'I tried getting closer, but it didn't help,' I say, 'though I did see the driver's face – he's got, er, really big eyebrows.

Oh, and the front left hubcap on the van was broken . . .'

The group exchange looks. It's obvious they're disappointed.

'Ah well,' Bear's mum says. 'At least he didn't see *you*, Maya.' She meets Drina's gaze.

'Exactly,' says Drina. 'If he'd seen you, things could have escalated; someone might have got hurt.'

'I'm sorry,' I mumble, feeling suddenly like I might be about to burst into tears. I turn away, not wanting Bear or his mums to see.

Drina clears her throat. 'Okay, gloves on then. Let's take a look at the packaging, see if that gives us any clues.' She turns to Rowan's dad. 'Will you lead the sample collection, Jake?'

Jake nods and everyone troops down the hill towards the stream, where most of the rubbish has piled up. As Rowan passes me she leans in and hisses: 'How useless do you have to be to get right up close to a van and still fail to take the reg number?' There's no mistaking the scathing tone to her voice.

I bite my lip, now feeling humiliated as well as upset. Rowan hurries away but I hang back, hoping no one will notice the shame on my face in the darkness. As I start walking again, Bear's mum comes over.

'Are you okay, sweetheart? It must have been terrifying

for you, earlier.' She puts her arm around my shoulders and squeezes me tight. Her hoodie is soft against my face. For a second it reminds me of hugging my own mum. She suddenly seems very far away, along with my whole life in London. Fresh tears spark in my eyes. I blink them back and draw away.

'I'm fine,' I say.

We walk down the hill to the stream. The group are spread out, gloves on, already rummaging carefully through the rubbish. Jake is handing out small tubes for the sample collection. The lights from all the torches glint on the metal drums. Drina nudges a large container with her foot.

'Every label torn off again, I see.' She crouches down and warily sniffs the container. 'I think this one had oil in it.'

'Nobody touch this one. I think it's some kind of acid,' says Jake, looking up from a big plastic bottle.

'Oils and acids are used in paper-making,' Bear's mum says.

'Could be that pulping place just outside Polborne,' John suggests.

'Or a paint factory,' CJ adds.

I wander among the strewn rubbish to where Bear is standing beside two large metal cans. I shine the light from my phone across a length of grubby plastic sheeting.

A tiny movement, just visible underneath it, catches my eye. I crouch down and gently lift the edge of the plastic.

A small, furry rabbit is scrabbling, helplessly at the grass. It yelps, clearly terrified. Only its front paws are moving. Its back and legs remain strangely, horribly still.

'Oh.' A sob rises inside me.

'What's up?' Bear squats down beside me.

I point to the rabbit. 'It was trapped under the sheeting. Something must have fallen on it. It can't move . . . oh, it's just a baby.' My voice cracks.

'The poor thing,' Bear says sadly. He examines the animal with gentle hands. 'One of the metal cans must have landed on it.'

I swallow hard, tears pricking at my eyes. 'What can we do?'

Bear shakes his head. 'Nothing. I think its back is broken.' He reaches out and, murmuring softly under his breath, gently strokes the rabbit's head. The animal's breathing calms and slows. 'At least it doesn't seem to be in too much pain.'

I reach out and rub the soft fur between the animal's ears. It nuzzles gently against my hand. The adult voices around us fade away as I watch the baby rabbit gradually stop moving. I've never seen anything dying before but somehow, instinctively, I know that's what I'm witnessing.

A few seconds that last an eternity tick away. The rabbit lets out its last breath and, suddenly all the life seeps out of it, leaving just fur and skin and bones. A tear trickles down my cheek. Together, Bear and I lift our hands from the creature's back.

'I'll take it to Drina. She'll bury it properly.' Bear picks up the rabbit and carries it across the grass. I'm about to follow him, when his mum materializes in front of me, bringing me back to the rubbish and the night and the group around me.

'We'll be leaving soon,' she says. 'We're loading CJ's car up with as much of the waste as we can. We'll come back when it's light and fetch the rest. Take it to a proper recycling place.'

'Right,' I say, not really listening.

Bear's mum touches my arm. 'Your mother does know you're out with us, doesn't she?' She smiles, anxiously, in the torchlight. 'I should have double-checked when you arrived.'

Over her shoulder I can see Bear talking to Drina. I can't hear what they're saying, but Drina's face is solemn as Bear hands over the baby rabbit.

'Of course Mum knows.' My throat tightens at the lie. I try to smile. 'She . . . she really supports what you're doing.'

'Good.' I'm sure I look guilty, but Bear's mum seems to believe me. 'Well, Bear and I will walk you home,' she goes on. 'Make sure you get safely back.'

Oh no! 'It's fine, there's no need,' I say quickly. 'You can leave me where I met Bear earlier, on the corner of Penwillick Wood and Polborne Road. That's just a few minutes from . . . from home.'

'Bear didn't meet you at your house?' His mum frowns. 'Where exactly are you staying?'

'Just past Penwillick,' I say, trying to remember what I've already told Bear. 'Off the main road.' As I speak, Bear reappears beside us.

'Oh, good, there you are,' his mum says. 'We're setting off now. CJ only has room for one person in his car, so we're going to walk. I've just been telling Maya, we'll make sure she gets safely home. All right?'

'Sure,' Bear says.

My stomach churns with anxiety as we set off. Bear and I quickly fall back, to the end of the line. We walk along in silence. Bear seems subdued, presumably because of the poor rabbit. My own thoughts dart between sadness for the little creature and terror that Bear and his family will find out I have lied about who I am — and where I live. What am I going to do? I can't let Bear and his mum walk me back to Gran's. Suppose they recognize her house?

Once they discover I live with her, all the other lies I've told are bound to come tumbling out too.

'Maya?'

I realize Bear has been speaking to me. 'Sorry?' I say. 'What was that?'

'I was just . . .' He lifts one shoulder in a self-conscious shrug. 'Would you like to meet up again on Saturday?'

My pulse quickens as he smiles at me, his eyes full of feeling in the moonlight.

I gaze back, so caught up in the moment that I forget my horror at the little rabbit's death as well as my terror of being outed as a Peyton.

'Sure,' I say, 'I'd like that.' The words hang briefly and delicately in the night air, before Bear takes my hand and we walk on, our palms lightly pressed together. For a minute or two I feel utterly happy . . . but then Penwillick Wood comes into view and all my fears surge back. If Bear finds out I've been lying to him, there's no way he'll ever want to see me again.

Ahead of us, his mum is speaking with Drina, pointing towards my supposed walk home. Any second now and she'll come over and I'll have to go with her and Bear and they'll realize I don't live where I said I did . . . which will lead to a whole bunch of fresh questions about where I *do* live.

I can't let that happen.

I let go of Bear's hand and take a step away. 'I'm going to go now,' I say.

'But Mum and I are walking you home,' he protests.

'I'd rather go alone.'

'But it's the middle of the night.'

'So?' I take another step. 'I know you're just trying to be nice, but I don't need a babysitter.' We stare at each other and I realize there's no explanation I can give that is going to make sense to him, so instead I just leap towards him, brush my lips against his cheek and whisper: 'See you Saturday.' Then I run, as fast as I can, not looking back or slowing down until I'm at the end of Gran's private road.

I glance over my shoulder to make sure no one has followed me. The coast is clear. I hurry on, towards Gran's house. I'm seeing Bear again soon, so it's not like I'll have ruined everything by running away. I should feel relieved but, as I slip, silently, back indoors, all I feel is an overwhelming sense of guilt. Why wasn't I honest with him from the start? The more I lie, the more I have to lie again. It's like I'm trapped by the untruths, as if they're the bars of a cage.

How on earth am I going to find my way out?

FIFTEEN

I toss and turn for ages before finally falling asleep, which means that when Gran wakes me up next morning I'm still groggy and tired.

'Not feeling well,' I mumble.

But Gran is having none of it. She feels my forehead with the back of her hand, then whips the duvet off my shoulders. 'Nothing wrong with you that a cup of tea and a slice of toast won't fix,' she says briskly.

I fall back to sleep as soon as she leaves the room. Five minutes later, I come to for a second time to find Leo shaking my shoulder.

'Gran says it's time to get up,' he says.

'Go away,' I mutter, pulling the duvet over my head.

'Where did you go last night?' Leo asks.

I whip the duvet away and stare at him. *How does he know?* 'What do you mean?' I demand.

Leo tilts his head to one side. 'I heard you coming up the stairs at 1.16 a.m.'

'I just went down for a glass of water,' I lie.

Leo looks me in the eye. 'No, you didn't,' he says.

'Like you know everything,' I bluster. 'Where else would I have gone?'

'I don't know,' Leo says, reasonably. 'But I know you didn't fetch a glass of water because –' he points to the bedside table – 'there *isn't* a glass of water.'

'Well, it's none of your business where I went,' I snap. 'And don't say anything to Gran.'

Leo considers this for a moment, then says, 'Okay,' and scuttles away.

I stumble out of bed and take a shower. Moments from last night keep running through my head: the terrifying seconds when the van driver was walking towards me and I had to hide; Bear's warm smile; Rowan's scathing voice . . . and that poor baby rabbit, the life fading out of it.

I try to push the whole night out of my mind, selecting sky-blue joggers and a simple white crop top for my day at the factory. A pair of smart white trainers and my big blue hoop earrings complete the outfit. I gaze at myself in the mirror and, not for the first time, wish I was a bit less ordinary-looking. What I'd give for Rowan's wild, dark, dramatic curls and piercing blue eyes.

'Maya!' Gran calls from downstairs. 'Hurry up!'

I grab my phone and make my way down to where Leo is shifting from side to side at the back door.

'Come on, Grandad,' he says, hopping on one leg now.

'All right, young man, let me get myself sorted.' Grandad is in the kitchen, tying the laces on his shoes.

Leo turns to me, eyes fizzing with excitement. 'The rockpoolers forum is saying there's a rock pool near here with some snakelocks anemones,' he announces. He's clearly put the fact that he called me out on a lie earlier completely out of his head. 'They use their tentacles to stun passing fish.'

'Gross.' I wrinkle my nose.

'I'm hoping to see some cushion starfish. They're my favourites,' Grandad calls out. 'And what do you say to a trip to the butterfly farm at Mawleggan afterwards?'

Leo nods eagerly. 'Okay!' I stare at him, surprised. I can't remember the last time I saw him this animated.

Gran appears from the kitchen with a slice of toast on a small plate. She thrusts it under my nose. 'Eat,' she commands.

Obediently, I take a bite from the toast. It's warm and nutty and slathered with butter. When Mum makes toast it's always white-sliced and served cold because she's doing ten other things at once.

Grandad and Leo disappear outside. Through the open back door, I watch Leo chattering happily as he trots across the grass.

'He seems settled and content, doesn't he?' Gran says.

I nod, finishing my toast. 'How did you get him away from his phone? At home he never stops playing games on it.'

Gran sighs. 'He just needed a little attention, somebody taking the trouble to *do* things with him.'

I gaze at her. Is that a dig at Mum? Gran doesn't sound angry. Just a little sad.

'Come on,' she says, checking her lipstick in the hall mirror and slipping a smart navy jacket on over her blouse. 'Let's go. I want you to tell me all about this new Peyton Rainbow range your uncle Harry's so excited about. He says you pretty much came up with the entire concept.'

It turns out to be my best day so far at Peyton Soaps. I get my first wage packet – and spend my entire tea break browsing for a new jacket. Meanwhile, the Julies are so impressed with my wrapping technique that I'm allowed to work on the gift bags and boxes. Just before lunch, Uncle Harry comes to get me and shows me the rough design for the Maya at Peyton Rainbow soap packaging. It's a block-colour wrap, with wide, bright blue stripes contrasting with thinner orange and red ones, and the name *Maya* written in swirly pink at the bottom.

'The designers have turned it around really fast. What do you think? Is it young enough? Cool enough?'

I tell Uncle Harry that I think the pink colour and the swirling lettering make the overall effect too girly, and he nods, chewing his lip thoughtfully.

'I think you're right. We'll go with something brighter and stronger.' He grins. 'It'll be a few more weeks before we get the pack design finalized, but we're going to put the first batch of the Maya soap into production very soon.'

'That's amazing,' I say.

'Well, it's all down to you.' Uncle Harry gazes across the open-plan office area. The only other person in here is Parvati, gathering papers at the far desk. 'Maya is going to make a brilliant brand designer one day,' he proclaims exuberantly.

Parvati smiles at us. 'I don't doubt it,' she says shyly, then scurries off to reception with her bundle of papers.

I wait till the door closes behind her then turn to Uncle Harry and say softly: 'Are you sure she's not your girlfriend? Because she *really* likes you.'

Uncle Harry lets out a low chuckle. 'You reckon?'

I nod.

'Nothing gets past you, does it.' He lowers his voice. 'The truth is that Parvati and I *did* have a thing, but . . .'

He makes a face. 'Well, it petered out. You know, just wasn't meant to be.'

'Ah,' I say. 'She does seems really nice.'

'Oh, she is,' Uncle Harry assures me. 'Now, I need to do a couple of emails before my next meeting. Why don't you take a break? Your gran'll be expecting you for lunch in ten minutes anyway.'

I leave him hunched over his computer and saunter into reception. Parvati is on a call. She waves at me, then turns back to the appointments book, saying: 'Next Wednesday is possible, but Thursday would be better.'

It's clouded over outside, a few drops of rain falling, so instead of going out to the car park, I take the door through to the corridor that leads to the loading area, where Leo hid from the bomb scare on our first day. I haven't been in this part of the factory since then and I immediately spot things I didn't notice before, including a cupboard close to the door. I peek inside, but there's nothing interesting here: just some boxes and a bucket of cleaning cloths and sprays. I close the door and wander towards the front of the loading bay. A worker in navy overalls is lugging a stack of cardboard boxes out onto the forecourt. He stops to take a swig from his thermos.

I'm about to go back into the main part of the factory, when a dark blue van trundles through the gate and parks on the tarmac just outside. The van's front left hubcap is broken, the metal over the wheel full of jagged edges. A wave of foreboding washes over me, as the driver opens the door and jumps out.

There's no mistaking those thick, dark eyebrows.

My stomach falls away. It's the man I saw dumping waste last night.

SIXTEEN

I shrink into the shadows, as the van driver walks towards the loading bay.

'Hey, Sam!' he calls out.

Sam looks up from his stack of cardboard boxes and waves a greeting. 'Hey, Matt! How are you?'

'Running late.' Matt grimaces. He glances at the boxes. 'Is this the delivery? Where's it going?'

'It's all on the transit note,' says Sam. He helps Matt haul the boxes into the van.

My mind reels. What is the driver from last night's dumping doing here, at Peyton Soaps? He isn't picking up waste materials. In fact, he's clearly delivering Peyton products.

Which must mean that he works for the company.

The men finish loading the van. Matt calls out his thanks, then drives off. Sam wipes his hands down his overalls and fetches a tupperware container from a nearby shelf. He leans against a stack of crates. As he takes a sandwich from his box, I step out of the shadows.

'Hi,' I say.

Sam looks up. 'Hi.' He looks at me vacantly, as if wondering what I'm doing here.

'I'm Maya, Ms Peyton's granddaughter.'

Sam nods, recognition settling on his face. 'Ah, hello.'

'Hi. I . . . er, I was just wondering . . . about the vans you use and, er, the drivers. Like the man who was just here?'

Sam takes a bite of his sandwich. 'What about 'em?' he asks.

'How do you know if they're going where they're supposed to?'

Sam shrugs. 'Guess we'd hear about it if they didn't.'

'Right . . .' I hesitate. 'That guy who just left . . . is he a Peyton Soaps employee?'

'Matt?' Sam makes a face. 'Reckon he is, yeah.'

'Was he here yesterday? Picking up rubbish?'

Sam shrugs again. 'Dunno. Not my shift.' He turns back to his sandwich, clearly indicating he doesn't want to talk any more.

I retreat into the shadows, feeling deeply uneasy. Was the waste we saw Matt dumping yesterday actually from Peyton Soaps? He might be an employee of Gran's, but that doesn't mean the containers and packaging were from here. Maybe he was using the van to transport someone else's rubbish.

I hurry along the corridor and through to reception, thinking hard. Parvati is on the phone again as I pass. She waves at me, motioning upwards with her finger. She's telling me to go upstairs for lunch with Gran in her office. It's the last thing I want to do. How can I face Gran when I don't know for sure if one of her employees is a criminal? Then Parvati covers the receiver with her hand and says: 'You just missed your gran. She asks if you'll wait up in her office while she sorts something on the factory floor. She'll only be ten minutes or so.'

'Thanks.' As I walk away it occurs to me that Gran's PC upstairs is more than likely to contain the company's employee files and van rosters. I have ten minutes to see what I can find out about Matt. I race through the open-plan office and up the short flight of steps to Gran's office. Her computer is on her desk and still open. I sit down in front of it and peer anxiously at the screen. The PC's desktop is as ordered as everything else in Gran's life. I find a folder called Staff, but inside it's just a bewildering list of files and spreadsheets. I scan them, mouth dry. There's too much information to take in properly. I close the folder and examine the desktop again.

There. I spot a spreadsheet entitled Waste Recycling Schedule. My fingers fumble on the keypad as I open it, only to find row upon row of numbers and abbreviations that I don't understand. *Wait*— I study the numbers in the left-hand column. Those are dates. Holding my breath I find the date for yesterday and track along the row: one of the cells contains the initials MA. It's also a link. I click on it and find myself staring at a pop-out file for Matt Alexander. Alongside his name and other staff details is a photo. It's definitely the man I saw last night.

I go back to the spreadsheet. There's a time next to Matt's initials – 16:40 – and, next to that, the letters EW. I click on these and the link takes me through to a scanned receipt headed with the company name: Evo Waste Ltd. This states that a delivery of industrial waste was made by Peyton Soaps at 17:04 yesterday afternoon.

The receipt is signed in two places. One of the signatures is clearly Matt Alexander's.

Footsteps sound on the stairs right outside.

Moving fast, I close the files and hurry away from Gran's desk to the window on the other side of the room. I'm staring through the glass, trying to make sense of what I've just read, as Gran sweeps inside.

'Some of Grandad's leftover quiche for lunch today,' she says cheerfully. 'All the more for us as Harry's out at a meeting. He's still singing your praises over the new collection, by the way.' Her voice sharpens: '*Maya?*'

I turn around and meet her gaze.

'What's the matter?' she asks, more softly.

'Nothing,' I lie. 'I . . . I was just watching someone pick up a load.' I hesitate. 'How do you know if your drivers are taking everything to the right place? You know . . . taking waste products to the proper recycling company rather than dumping it somewhere?'

Gran stares at me. 'Why would they do that?' she asks. 'Evo Waste is only a short drive away. And it's not the *drivers* who pay the recycling company to take the waste, so it's not like they'd be saving money by *not* delivering it. *I'm* the one who pays them. And very expensive it is too. Plus we get signed receipts for each load.'

I nod, remembering the scanned receipt I saw just now. But it doesn't add up. Could the rubbish we saw Matt dumping last night have come from somewhere else? Just because the man has a job at Peyton Soaps doesn't mean he couldn't work for someone else on the side.

'Why d'you ask, anyway? What's going on, Maya?'

'Nothing.' I force down a mouthful of quiche then glance at Grandad's message for today.

Life is either a daring adventure or nothing at all.

It's the final spur I need. After wolfing down my lunch,

I tell Gran I'm going outside for some fresh air. She kisses me on the cheek and turns to the mountain of papers on her desk.

Once outside, I take out my phone and find the number. My voice trembles as my call is answered by a bored-sounding woman:

'How may I help you?' she intones.

'I . . . er . . .' I clear my throat. 'Er, I'm trying to confirm if a waste, er, consignment came to you from us yesterday? The delivery driver was Matt Alexander and it would have been signed for just after five p.m.'

'Hold, please.'

A tinny tune floats down the line as I wait, my mobile hot against my ear. I'm on the shady side of the car park; the big doors through to the factory floor are right opposite. Two weeks ago, I watched the staff flooding through those doors after the bomb scare. I can hardly believe how much has happened since then.

The seconds tick past, and then the woman is back.

'Sorry to keep you, but no, we didn't receive anything with that driver's name. Which company was he coming from again?'

'Peyton Soaps.' My voice is hoarse. 'I thought . . . don't you have a contract with them?' I ask, my voice hoarse.

Another pause, then the woman speaks again. 'No, we

haven't had a contract with Peyton's for almost a year.'

Almost a year?

'Ah, I see,' I stammer. 'Thank you.' I ring off, my head spinning.

If Evo Waste Ltd didn't receive the Peyton Soaps waste yesterday afternoon, then Matt Alexander *must* have dumped it last night. But why would he do that? What would he have to gain?

Like Gran said: *It's not the drivers who pay the recycling company to take the waste . . . I'm the one who pays them. And very expensive it is too.*

Cold fingers reach around my heart, squeezing tight. There's only one possible explanation: Gran is cutting costs. She's getting her staff to dump industrial waste, then faking receipts and payments so that it looks like she's properly recycling it!

I'm no expert, obviously, but I'm certain *all* of that is illegal – as well as totally immoral. Which means that Gran, for all her insistence on how green she has made her company, is a greedy, planet-destroying hypocrite.

SEVENTEEN

It's only the thought of meeting Bear tomorrow that keeps me going for the rest of the day. I'm quiet back at Gran and Grandad's, joining in with the usual board games but without much enthusiasm. Luckily Leo more than makes up for my lack of excitement. He chatters away about how well he's doing at Go and Cluedo, then tells us about his trip with Grandad earlier to the butterfly farm.

'There were *loads* of Painted Ladies,' he informs me. 'I counted three hundred and forty-one just in the first *hour*.'

Gran and Grandad laugh and I force a smile onto my face, just so they don't ask me again if I'm all right.

Truth is, I'm very far from all right. How can Gran smile and laugh like that, while behind everyone's backs she's flouting the law, polluting the countryside and – worst of all – destroying wildlife by dumping Peyton's waste?

I can't get the image of the poor terrified dying rabbit out of my head. And it's all Gran's fault.

I hate her.

I go to bed early, but lie awake for ages. I try to distract myself by thinking about what's going on back in London. Caroline Abara's fashion-show-themed 'come in your most out-there outfit' party is this weekend. The old me from a few days ago would have been totally miserable at missing it.

Right now a party like that seems completely pointless. Who cares about fashion when your family is rotten to the core?

It's a relief to leave the house the next morning and make my way across the beach to meet Bear. I've already decided I'm not going to tell him what I've found out about Peyton Soaps' corruption. Not yet, anyway. For now I just want to forget about everything to do with Gran and the family business, put the lies I've told him to the back of my mind and enjoy spending time together.

The sun is shining as I reach our meeting place at the edge of the trees. Bear is already there, Skye at his side.

'She insisted on coming,' he says with a smile.

I grin at her. She's dressed today in a pink tunic with purple leggings and trainers with a kitten face on the toes.

'Cool shoes,' I say.

Skye beams at me as if I'd announced she was my favourite person in the whole world. She skips on ahead of us, back to the camp. As we walk, I sneak a sideways glance at Bear. He's dressed in long shorts and a T-shirt. There's a leather thong around his neck and he's wearing battered leather sandals on his feet.

'How come you wear leather?' I ask. 'I thought you'd be against stuff that comes from animals?'

Bear shakes his head. Through the trees, the sun catches the highlights in his blond hair. I stare at his oval face, with his long, sloped nose and high cheekbones. He's so good-looking it's kind of ridiculous.

'Our priority is wearing clothes that already exist,' he explains. 'There's so much stuff already out there. We did this research project for home school and I couldn't believe it – apparently, the fashion industry creates ten per cent of the world's greenhouse gas emissions.'

'No way!' I glance down at my Bonropa all-in-one playsuit. I got it at the start of the summer for just a few pounds. It's such a pretty blue colour and, up until this minute, it was one of my favourite outfits. But maybe wearing it makes *me* part of the problem Bear is talking about.

'Do you hate me for buying new stuff?' The question blurts out of me.

Bear turns to me, surprised. 'Of course not. *You're* not the problem. The problem is the powerful companies and people in charge who aren't looking after the planet.'

We walk on in silence to the camp. Rowan is sitting outside the longhouse when we walk up, her long legs stretched out in front of her. Two little boys are playing with a football nearby. They're in matching red shorts and have the same wild, dark curls as Rowan and her dad. They must be her brothers. Skye has already gone over to them and is kicking the ball.

Rowan scrambles to her feet when she sees us. She's dressed in the faded jumpsuit that she was wearing when I first met her. I remember her scathing put-down on the night of the waste dump and brace myself for another scornful outburst, but, to my surprise, she gives me a rueful smile.

'Hi, Maya. I'm sorry I was so rude the other night,' she says. 'I was just upset that we didn't get the van's registration number, but it wasn't your fault and I shouldn't have taken it out on you.'

I stare at her, taken aback. 'Oh,' I say, remembering what Drina said at the time. 'Er, thanks, but I shouldn't have risked being seen like that. It wasn't fair on everyone else.'

'It's just so annoying that we're back at square one.' Rowan sighs.

I nod, slowly. Now I'm here it feels weird not explaining everything I know.

'What is it?' Rowan's sharp eyes fix on mine like she can see right through me.

'Nothing,' I say. 'What . . . what would you do if you *did* know who the van belonged to?'

'I guess we'd try to find out whether the driver was acting on his own or whether the company who produced the waste told him to dump it,' Bear says. 'Then we'd pass on the information to the police and the environmental agencies—'

'Who most likely wouldn't do much,' Rowan adds, with a grimace. 'So we'd probably do something ourselves.'

'Oh?' I try to sound casual. 'Like what sort of "something"?'

'Peaceful protest of some kind,' Bear says.

'So . . . so no one would get hurt?' I ask.

'Of course not,' Bear says.

There's a pause. Sun filters through the trees and the breeze feels soft and warm on my face. I sense Rowan staring at me and look down.

'What is it, Maya?' she asks. 'What aren't you telling us?'

My cheeks burn. I'm sure my face is bright red, but I force myself to meet her gaze.

Rowan frowns. 'Do you know something about the van driver?'

I hesitate, feeling torn.

'Maya?' Bear asks.

'Did you recognize him?' Rowan's eyes widen. 'Is he from that place you're working at, from Peyton Soaps?'

I look down at my toes again, my heart thudding. The tips of Bear's worn leather sandals and Rowan's faded canvas pumps are just in view, harmonizing perfectly with the dry dusty earth outside the longhouse. In contrast, my own trainers gleam bright and white.

'Maya?' Rowan persists. 'Was that man dumping rubbish for Peyton Soaps?'

What should I say? I don't want to betray Gran, but hasn't she already betrayed me? She's lied about making her company – the business that bears my own family name – environmentally friendly. And she's actively damaging the planet that she says she cares about.

I look up. I look from Rowan to Bear. And, as I gaze into his serious, green eyes, I know that I can't lie to him again.

I take a deep breath.

'Yes,' I say. 'Peyton Soaps are the ones dumping the waste.'

EIGHTEEN

Rowan and Bear stare at me.

'Are you sure about this?' Rowan demands.

'Yes.' I pause. It's right to tell them what I found out, but it isn't easy. 'I didn't know it was them until yesterday. I saw the van driver when I was at work. He's a Peyton Soaps employee.'

Rowan's jaw drops.

'Wait,' Bear says. 'Was the guy actually dumping waste *for* Peyton Soaps? Or did he take their money and then dump it?'

'The driver doesn't handle the money,' I say. 'Waste recycling is paid for by the company. But Peyton Soaps are only pretending to pay.'

'How do you know?' Rowan asks.

'I was at work and I snuck into G—, er, Ms Peyton's office to look on her computer.'

'Seriously?' Bear's eyes widen.

I explain how I found the signed receipt from Evo Waste, then called and discovered it was a fake. 'Peyton

Soaps hasn't actually sent any recycling to Evo Waste in almost a year.'

'Wow! You did all that?' Bear's expression is somewhere between amazed and impressed.

Rowan whistles. 'This means the company's responsible for dumping *masses* of industrial waste.' She gives me a determined look. 'I'm telling my dad. And Drina. We need to act.'

She rushes off. I stare at Bear, my stomach twisting with anxiety.

He studies me carefully. 'Do you feel bad about telling us?' he asks.

'It's just, Ms Peyton's been so good to me and . . . and my mum,' I falter, hating myself for not just coming out with it and confessing the whole truth.

'I get that,' Bear says, 'but what she's doing is wrong.'

'I know.' I shuffle awkwardly from foot to foot.

Bear points to the longhouse. 'Come on, let's get a drink,' he suggests, and I follow him inside.

The longhouse is basically a large, oblong room, dominated by a long, central table with benches on either side. Light from the open windows floods in, casting shadows over the wooden floor. John and CJ are standing in the kitchen area at the far end of the room, examining a batch of potatoes laid out on the counter. CJ's lank brown hair falls over his face as he picks up a tray of knobbly-looking carrots and sets them down next to the potatoes. He looks up as Bear walks over to the fridge and he waves a greeting to us both.

I smile and wave back, then wander over to the window. Outside, on the sunlit earth, Skye and Rowan's little brothers have been joined by another two boys and a slightly older girl. The girl is organizing everyone into teams for a football match. I watch them, feeling envious. When you're little, life is simple. You don't have to untangle complicated lies or grapple with big decisions about doing the right thing.

Bear reappears with two glasses of cloudy apple juice. We sit down at the end of the trestle table. The corner of the longhouse is full of logs, piled high next to the unlit wood burner. I can just imagine how cosy it gets in here in the winter.

I take a sip of apple juice. 'Delicious,' I say.

'I helped make it,' Bear says proudly.

As he speaks, Drina and Bear's mum walk in, with Rowan and her dad, Jake. The four of them sit – Rowan on Bear's other side, the three adults opposite us. Across the room, John and CJ peer in our direction, clearly wondering what we're all there to discuss.

Drina clears her throat and fixes me with her clear,

sharp eyes. 'Rowan says you have some information for us, Maya?'

I take a deep breath and go over my story again, leaving nothing out except my real connection to Peyton Soaps. As I speak, John and CJ draw nearer, listening intently. Drina keeps her gaze fixed on me as I talk, shushing Rowan's dad, Jake, when he tries to interrupt. Once I'm done, she sits back.

'That was quick thinking to check the waste schedule,' she says, 'and gutsy of you to make the call to the waste recycling company.'

'Your mum must be so proud of you,' Bear's mum says. 'You know, if you need more help with her, I volunteer with a local caregivers' group. We might be able to organize some respite care for you.'

'Oh.' I look down, unable to meet her eyes. 'Thank you, but, er, we're fine.'

'So what now?' CJ asks from the end of the table. 'What do we do with the information Maya's brought us?'

'Well,' Drina says, 'we can tell the police—'

'Who will say they'll look into it,' says Jake, rolling his eyes, 'but who won't make it much of a priority.'

'That would make Maya a whistleblower,' Bear's mum points out. She looks along the table, a worried expression on her face, then turns to me. 'You'd have to tell the police what you saw on the company computer.'

'Oh.' My heart starts drumming, fast, against my ribs. 'It's just . . . if Ms Peyton knows I've done that, I'll lose my summer job, which I've only got because she wanted to help me and mum.'

'Couldn't it be an anonymous call?' Rowan asks.

'Then the police would make it even less of a priority,' her dad grumbles.

'Plus, if Peyton Soaps know they're being investigated, they can easily get rid of the documents that prove their guilt,' Drina adds.

'Not to mention do an internal investigation into who leaked the data,' Bear's mum says. 'We can't put a child in that position.'

'Of course we can't,' Drina says. 'Obviously not.'

I glance around, feeling relieved.

'No wonder that Peyton woman launched that appeal against us,' Drina continues. 'She must really want us gone.' She shakes her head. 'It's all so cynical: greenwashing her company, thinking she's above the law, not a care for the consequences of her actions.'

I stare at my lap, certain someone will see the awkwardness in my expression if I lift my face. There's a general murmuring of agreement, then CJ clears his throat. Everyone looks at him. CJ rubs his hand over the reddish-brown stubble on his chin. There's an impatience in his eyes.

'So what *are* we going to do?' he asks. 'We have to do *something*.'

Drina nods. 'I think, under the circumstances, we're perfectly entitled to take some kind of direct action.'

'Um . . .' I stammer. All eyes turn in my direction. It takes every bit of courage I have to speak: 'I don't want you to hurt anyone.'

'Of course not.' Bear's mum pats my hand.

'We wouldn't,' Bear says beside me. 'We'd never do anything violent.'

'That's right. We don't break any laws, Maya,' Drina says, nodding fiercely. 'Or risk hurting people or property. But CJ's right. We need to make a stand.'

'What does that mean?' I ask.

'It means,' Drina says, a smile curving her mouth and making her eyes twinkle with mischief, 'it means that we're going to give Peyton Soaps a taste of their own medicine.'

NINETEEN

Monday morning arrives and I'm wound up with nerves.
Will the Harmony Earth Group have actually carried out
Drina's plan? I've been thinking about nothing else for
nearly forty-eight hours. Naturally, Gran's sharp eyes have
noticed how distracted I've been, but I think she's bought
my explanation that I'm missing my London friends.

Eight a.m. and I'm downstairs early for once, which
means I'm right there when the call from work comes.

'Hello, Parvati,' Gran answers in her usual, crisp tone.
Then her voice lowers to a growl: 'You can't be serious . . .'

Grandad looks up and even Leo stops talking mid-
sentence.

I watch Gran's horrified face, a slice of toast halfway
to my mouth. Moments later, she is off the phone and
picking up her jacket from the back of her chair.

'What's the matter?' Grandad asks.

'Tell you later,' Gran mouths, glancing at Leo, as if to
say, *I don't want to explain in front of him.* Grandad nods.
Gran turns to me. 'We need to leave right now, Maya.

Are you ready? You can stay home if—'

'I'm ready,' I say, putting down my toast.

Before we get into the car, Gran sends Uncle Harry a text to call her as soon as he's up. Along the way, she explains what has happened; it sounds as if everything has gone exactly as Drina planned. Even so, I'm not prepared for the sight that greets us as we approach Peyton Soaps.

At least half of the rubbish we found off the Polborne Road last week is strewn across the car park entrance: a mess of dented metal, broken-up cardboard and plastic canisters. I gaze at a length of stained plastic sheeting. Is that the one the poor rabbit was trapped under? I shudder at the memory.

Gran parks, her lips pressed angrily together. We get out of the car in silence. Parvati rushes out of the building, Artem striding after her.

'I can't believe this . . . Oh, Ms Peyton, isn't it awful? . . . What a mess!' Parvati cries.

'I've called the police,' Artem says, grimly.

'Good.' Gran nods. 'Now, first things first – do you think there's any hazardous material in there? Do we need to evacuate?'

'I don't think so,' Artem replies. 'It looks like every container has had its label removed and been washed out.' He curls his lip. 'Deliberately done, I'm sure, so that we can't trace what was inside them.'

My heart sinks. I know, in fact, that Drina ordered all the cans to be rinsed out to make sure they didn't pose any danger.

'Why would anyone do this?' Parvati asks.

I look away.

'Has anyone claimed responsibility?' Gran asks. 'Have you checked the security cameras?'

'Yes. There's nothing on film.' Artem indicates the three cameras, each one positioned just above an exit point. 'None of the footage has captured anything going on this far away in the car park.'

Parvati hands Gran a folded-over piece of paper. 'This was left for you, Ms Peyton,' she says.

'Right,' Gran says grimly. She fishes out her glasses and flips open the note. Standing beside her, I read:

This is YOUR rubbish.
Next time deal with it ethically,
legally and sustainably.
We are watching.

Gran clenches her jaw, the muscles twitching under her skin. 'Oh, for heaven's sake! I bet this is the work of that awful group in the woods,' she spits. 'Now they're trying to make out I'm some sort of local polluter!'

I look down at my feet.

'But all our waste is recyled,' Parvati exclaims, reading over Gran's shoulder. 'What are they talking about?'

'I have no idea,' Gran mutters.

I stare at her, a chill running through me. How is she capable of telling such barefaced lies?

Gran's phone rings. I can see from the screen that it's Uncle Harry. She walks away to take the call. Parvati gazes at me, looking bewildered.

'I don't understand why people would do this,' she says, numbly.

'At least they didn't break in and damage any machinery. And they didn't hurt anyone,' I point out.

'True,' Parvati says with a sniff. She puts her arm across my shoulders. 'I can't bear to look at it all,' she says, waving towards the rubbish. 'Let's go and make everyone a tea.'

I follow her into the building. It's horrible seeing how upset Parvati is, but it will all have been worth it if Gran has learned her lesson. And surely she must have done now? She can't possibly think Peyton Soaps can carry on illegally dumping its waste, now that she's been caught out so publicly.

I close my eyes, praying that the next time I see Bear all this will be behind us and I can just enjoy our time together.

I hover beside Parvati, helping fetch mugs and milk. As she makes tea, more and more staff arrive. Everyone walks in with wide eyes and horrified expressions. Soon the open-plan office is crammed with people angrily discussing the rubbish outside. Nobody looks remotely interested in starting work but, after twenty minutes or so, Gran appears and calls for silence. She stands on the steps that lead up to her private office and speaks, calmly and seriously stating that she has reported the 'disgusting dumping' to the police.

'We are a responsible, ethical company,' she says. 'Our waste water is properly treated, our manufacturing processes are as green as possible, and our packaging is sustainably recycled by Evo Waste, a reputable local waste management company.'

Anger burns inside me.

What a liar.

'I'd like you all to know that I've hired a professional team to clear up the mess outside. In the meantime, our best response to the misinformed cowards who left it on our doorstep is to get back to work as soon as possible.' Her voice rises. 'Getting on with our jobs and our lives is the best way to show them that their intimidatory tactics will never win.'

'Hear, hear!' Uncle Harry steps forward, clapping his

hands furiously. All the staff join in for a moment, then the crowd disperses. Soon almost everyone has followed Artem through to the factory floor. Only Gran, Uncle Harry and Parvati are left in the open-plan office. The three of them draw together in a huddle.

Nobody is paying me any attention.

I scurry up to Gran's office, my head reeling, and stare at her computer. It's powered down. I touch the keyboard and a password request pops up. It's hopeless – I have no idea what Gran's password might be. If only I could get into her files again I could message myself copies of the fake receipts and expose her fraud myself. *Except* . . . I gasp. I don't need the receipts. The receptionist at Evo Waste told me that Peyton no longer uses their company. Gran literally just said the opposite to the entire factory. That, by itself, is proof she is lying. All I need to do to prove it is record a conversation with Evo Waste. Then I'll confront Gran with the recording and she'll be caught out in the lie. No defence.

Surely that will shame her into ending all this?

I peek around the door to check downstairs: Parvati, Gran and Uncle Harry are still deep in conversation in the office below. Beyond them, I can already hear the low hum of the machinery starting up in the factory.

I go back into Gran's private office and shut the door.

I take out my mobile, download a call-recording app, then dial Evo Waste.

The bored-sounding receptionist I spoke to before answers: 'You're through to Evo Waste. How may I help you?'

'Hi,' I say, my mouth dry. 'I rang the other day, about Peyton Soaps, and . . . and I was wondering if you could confirm something for me.'

'Yes?'

I clutch my phone, my fingers cold and clammy. 'You said before that you haven't had a contract with Peyton's for almost a year. Is that right?

'Ah,' says the woman, a note of embarrassment creeping into her voice. 'It seems I was wrong about that. I've just been told by our managing director that in fact we *do* have a contract with Peyton Soaps.'

'Oh?' For a fraction of a second, my heart leaps. Perhaps this whole business has been one big mix-up. 'Your managing director?'

'Yes,' the woman says. 'Nicholas Ashley. He said that if anyone asks, I should make it clear that there *is*, in fact, a long-standing contract with Peyton's. Mr Ashley is dealing with all their files personally. That's why I didn't know before. Mr Ashley only explained all this fifteen minutes ago.'

My stomach contracts, like I've been winded. 'He told you that fifteen minutes ago?'

'Yes. I'm sorry for the earlier misunderstanding. Is there anything else?'

'No,' I say. 'Thank you.'

I ring off and sink into the chair opposite Gran's desk. All the hope that surged inside me just moments before drains away to nothing. Gran must have called the Evo Waste MD this morning and got him to lie on her behalf. Which means she's capable not only of fraud and waste dumping, but of covering up her crimes too.

I lean forward, my head in my hands.

It's so wrong. Gran clearly has every intention of carrying on her illegal activities, even though it means hurting wildlife and the environment, lying to everyone she knows and betraying every principle she claims to live by.

I am going to stop her. Whatever it takes.

TWENTY

I find Gran and tell her I'd like to go home for the rest of the day. Normally, when people ask for time off, she purses her lips and mutters something about 'commitment' and 'work ethic'. However, today she's so distracted by the litter dump that she simply nods and says: 'Good idea, Maya, good idea.'

Parvati calls me a taxi and and I arrive home shortly before midday, just as Grandad and Leo are leaving to go rock-pooling. Alone in the house, I hurry upstairs. I can't stay here, weighed down by what I know about Gran. Bear and the rest of the group need to know that their plan failed, that Gran is not only still lying but also completely unrepentant. The last remnants of loyalty I felt for her vanished when I realized she'd got Evo Waste to cover for her lies.

I hesitate in front of my wardrobe, determined to avoid wearing anything that looks cheaply produced. After a ten-minute rummage, I decide that this is basically impossible given the clothes I own. I compromise by changing into my oldest pair of non-denim shorts and a plain grey T-shirt that I bought just a couple of months ago, but which already looks a hundred years old.

Half an hour later and I'm on the woodland path that leads to the eco camp. I reach Bear's house and knock on the door. No one answers. As I turn away, Bear himself appears, strolling into the clearing. Rowan and the camp visitor, CJ, are a few metres behind him, deep in conversation. Bear's eyes register surprise as he sees me.

'Maya, are you okay?'

'I'm fine. I just . . .' I stop. Now I'm actually here, it's harder than I thought it would be to talk about what Gran has done. At least, hard to do it without slipping up and revealing I'm her granddaughter.

'What's up?' Rowan has seen me now as well and is hurrying over, CJ at her side. 'Were you at work earlier? How did they react?'

I gaze at each face in turn: Bear's is full of concern and Rowan's all curiosity. CJ's expression I can't read. His eyes are guarded, as if he's weighing me up, his lips set in a hard, thin line.

'Everyone at Peyton Soaps was upset . . . about all the rubbish,' I stammer, hoping that Bear will read in my eyes and voice that I want to speak to him privately.

Bear just frowns.

'And?' Rowan demands. 'Did Ms Peyton accept it was *their* waste?'

I shake my head.

Rowan turns to CJ. 'That's what you said would happen.'

'It's because we haven't properly hit them where it hurts.' CJ curls his lip. 'A few empty cans and bottles at the entrance to the car park isn't enough. It doesn't stop production; it doesn't affect profits.' He pauses. 'We need to go further.'

Rowan nods eagerly.

I glance at Bear, still hoping he'll see how much I'd prefer to talk to him on his own. But Bear isn't looking at me. He's staring at CJ, a worried look in his eyes.

'As far as I'm concerned, we need to take direct action against Peyton Soaps,' Rowan announces, her hands on her hips.

'Absolutely.' CJ makes a fist. He sounds very sure of himself. 'I'd go so far as to say we have to take invasive action.'

What does *that* mean?

I shuffle nervously from side to side. Bear catches my eye at last. He gives a tiny shake of his head, then turns to CJ.

'We only do peaceful protests here, CJ,' he says. 'We

don't want to hurt anyone.'

'Bear's right,' I add quickly. 'We need to stop the company dumping waste illegally, but it's not fair to punish the people who work there. It's not their fault.'

'True,' Rowan acknowledges. 'But still . . . we have to do *something*. Something *big*.'

CJ lifts his head and looks around the clearing, presumably making sure the four of us are alone. His voice is low and intense as he says: 'We absolutely don't hurt anyone, but that doesn't mean we shouldn't slow down production.' A smile twists across his mouth. 'We should do something at the factory that loses them *money*. You know, makes a difference to their bottom line. *That*'ll make them think twice about dumping waste illegally again.'

'Mum and Drina wouldn't go for that,' Bear says. 'Especially not if it meant breaking into the factory.'

'Neither would my dad,' Rowan adds.

CJ shrugs. 'Who says we have to tell them?'

'You're kidding,' Bear says. 'I—'

'What exactly are you thinking of doing?' Rowan interrupts.

'Soap needs to be made with purified water, right?' CJ says.

I nod. 'They use fresh bottles every day.'

'So what would happen if "by accident" they used some of the water that Peyton Soaps pollutes instead?'

'You mean switch containers?' Rowan's eyes widen. 'That's *perfect*.'

I exchange looks with Bear. He still looks uncertain.

CJ turns to me. 'You work there, right?'

'Yes, but I don't have a key or anything.'

'Then the first step is for you to get one, so the three of us –' he points to Rowan, Bear and himself – 'have access to the storage room while the building is empty.'

I stare at him. Is he serious?

'It's not just the key,' I bluster. 'There's an alarm and . . . and security cameras.'

CJ shrugs. 'Then you need to work out how to get us past the alarm, too. I can deal with the cameras myself.'

My heart thuds. CJ must see the fear on my face. 'I know it's a lot,' he says, 'but it's the only way. We need to hit them hard and we need to hit them soon. Before the end of the week.'

'I'm still not sure . . .' Bear says, hesitantly.

'*I* am,' Rowan interrupts. She draws herself up, excitement sparking in her eyes.

'Once we're in the storage room,' says CJ, 'we take one of the bottles of distilled water that's in there and switch it for the dirty water we've brought with us. We leave the polluted water close to the door, so it will get used the next day.' He grins. 'We'll be in and out in less than ten minutes. Job done.'

There's a long pause. My guts twist. It's a good plan but it's risky. And I've got no idea how I'll be able to carry out my part of it.

'How do you feel about this, Maya?' Bear asks. 'Stealing keys and working out alarms is a lot to ask.'

'Bear's right – that's why Maya shouldn't come with us on the night we attack,' CJ says. 'Helping us beforehand though . . . well, that's your choice, Maya. How badly do you want to make a difference? How much are you prepared to *dare*?' He stresses the last word.

The three of them look at me, Bear anxious, Rowan eager, CJ watchful.

'So what do you say, Maya?' CJ asks eventually. 'Are you up for it?'

I take a deep breath. 'Yes,' I say. 'It's the only way. *Yes*.'

TWENTY-ONE

I already know where Gran keeps the slim, metal master key for the main factory door, but there's no way I'll be able to steal it. Like everything with Gran, the key is part of a highly organized system and kept securely with her other keys in her handbag, which never leaves her side.

Uncle Harry, on the other hand, just tosses his keys into a bowl on the kitchen counter of his flat. That evening, when Leo and I pop over for another game of Bumper Bonanza, I surreptitiously check the bowl while Uncle Harry sets up his big TV. Sure enough, the key to the main entrance of Peyton Soaps is there. Harry's *never* first to work, so never needs to use it. I'm certain he won't spot if it's missing. Fingers trembling, I slide it, silently, off the bunch and shove it into my pocket.

So far so good.

CJ texts me on Tuesday morning to ask how I'm getting on. I explain that I have a key but, as yet, no idea how to get him past the alarm.

You'll work it out, CJ messages back. *You've got till*

Thursday evening. That's when we do the job.

The day passes in a blur. Gran – still claiming to be baffled and outraged at being accused of illegal dumping – has got Parvati to go over the company's waste protocols. Gran wants her to come up with a list of what she calls 'Peyton's Green Principles', that she can try and use for PR. What a nerve!

I ask a few questions about the alarm, but only discover what I already suspected: each of the three entry points to the building – the loading bay, the reception and the fire door into the factory – has an alarm, activated by a code, that is switched on when everyone leaves the building.

The next day, I'm determined to find out more. I dress for work in my Barata joggers and a stripy crop top, eat the toast Gran puts in front of me, then get into her car. Gran chats away as we drive to the factory, but I say very little. I have to make progress today.

Part of the problem is that there are only a few people with the information I need. Most of the staff walk in through reception once it's open. They sign in for work at an automated stand next to Parvati's desk. They certainly don't have anything to do with setting or turning off the alarm system. Parvati must know the code for the alarm because she gets to work before everyone else. Gran probably knows the sequence too, but I can't imagine many other people at Peyton Soaps do. I could ask one of them outright but, if I do, I'll look super guilty later on, after the dirty water switch is uncovered.

Gran drops me at reception. I'm hoping Parvati will give me a job working alongside her, which will allow me to ask some carefully casual and indirect questions about the alarm. But she says there's nothing I can help with at the moment and shoos me away to the factory floor.

The soap-making machines are already in full swing, churning out strips of soap and filling the air with the sharp scent of pine. The fire door that leads outside is shut – as it has been every time I've ever seen it, apart from that one time during the bomb scare on my first day.

Floor manager Artem is in the doorway of the stockroom. As soon as he sees me lurking he barks: 'Maya! Come here, please. I'd like you to take a message to Parvati.' He sounds cross.

'Er, okay.' I walk over. The stockroom is crammed with containers of all shapes and sizes, some made of metal, some plastic. I stare at the huge plastic bottles of distilled water at the front and think about CJ's plan. My insides contract.

'What's the message?' I ask.

Artem scowls. 'Remind Parvati that she still hasn't

updated our stock records even though I've been asking for weeks.' He points to the rows of huge aluminium canisters to the right of the stockroom. 'See those vegetable oil containers? They are in here, but *not* on the computer system.' I stare at him blankly. He lets out an exasperated sigh and points to the big plastic bottles at the front. 'But *here*, there is less distilled water than what the computer says we should have, and *here* –' he waves to the tightly packed containers behind – 'it's all sodium hydroxide. Hardly any potassium hydroxide at all.'

I follow his gaze. When Artem showed me the full soap-making process, I learned that an essential step is the mixing of highly flammable hydroxide – or lye – with purified water. 'Remind me, why do you need both the hydroxides?' I ask.

Artem rolls his eyes. 'Potassium for liquid soap. Sodium for solid soap. Now, please let Parvati know she must urgently update the system.' He glares at me.

I scuttle back to Parvati. She makes a face when I pass on Artem's message.

'Yes, I know the inventory system needs a complete overhaul,' she says. 'I just haven't had time—' At this point the phone rings and she breaks off to answer it.

Frustrated, I return to the factory floor. Artem spots me instantly and directs me over to help with packaging.

Obediently I trot around to the packaging station, where a huge new batch of lavender and sandalwood soaps stand on trolleys, ready to wrap. Each bar has to be individually encased in wax paper, then tied with lilac or pale-yellow ribbons. I lay out the ribbons, like the Julies showed me last week, then get to work. The girl who looked down her nose at me on my first day is stationed beside me, her nimble fingers tying bows far faster than mine.

'Hi,' I say, determined to be friendly. 'It's Hayley, right?'

Hayley glances across at me. She has a thin, pinched face and a straggly blond ponytail. 'That's right,' she says, swishing her hair off her shoulder. She gives me a withering look. 'And we all know who you are.'

I frown. 'Sorry?'

Hayley purses her lips. 'Look, lots of people won't say it, but I'm not afraid: you only got this job because of your gran. There's plenty of people without work in Penwillick. It's not fair.'

'It's . . . it's just a temporary summer job,' I stammer.

'Whatever.' Hayley sniffs. 'I suppose you'll be creeping off to your gran and getting me the sack now I've spoken my mind.'

'No, I won't,' I say, stung. 'And for your information,

I didn't *ask* for this job. My gran *made* me work here. So you're not the only one who wasn't happy about it.' Face flushed, I turn back to my wrapping.

After a while, I sense Hayley watching me and look up again.

'What is it now?' I demand.

'Did you try telling your gran you didn't want the job?' she asks.

I roll my eyes. 'What do you think? She's not exactly the easiest person to talk out of something when her mind's made up.'

'True.' Hayley laughs, which makes her face so much lighter and warmer that I find myself smiling back.

'Anyway,' I say, 'I actually like it here now. A lot.'

'You don't miss London?' Hayley asks.

'Not really,' I say truthfully.

Hayley launches into a series of questions about city life – mostly involving shops and shows I've never heard of. She talks non-stop, seemingly undeterred by my limited answers. At last she pauses, moving on in her wrapping to a series of gift sets.

I take my chance to ask the question that's been circling at the back of my head. 'If I ever had to come in early . . .' I start.

Hayley snorts. 'Why would *you* have to do that?'

'If, like, my gran wanted some extra work done,' I say, thinking fast. 'She's just as fierce with me as she is with everyone else, you know.'

'Really?' Hayley says, then she grins. 'She *is* a bit strict.'

'Exactly,' I say. 'Anyway, if I came in before everyone else, could I use the fire door that leads straight into the factory?'

'Not without a dongle,' Hayley explains.

My ears prick up. 'A dongle?'

'Yeah, Artem has one. It's like a small black sensor. You just wave it at the number pad and . . .'

'And it opens the door?' I ask, my excitement mounting. 'Automatically?'

Hayley nods.

'What about the alarm? Does this, er, dongle thing stop that going off?'

Hayley shrugs. 'I guess.'

'Oh,' I say. 'Thanks.' I turn back to my wrapping, trying to look and sound super casual, but inside my heart is pounding.

I finish the tray of sandalwood soaps I'm working on then, murmuring to Hayley that I need the bathroom, I set off through the factory. The glass-walled saponification room is busy with workers in masks. That means they must be mixing lye with water – it's dangerous to breathe in the fumes. I spot Artem, busy at the machines. He hasn't noticed me.

I make my way across the factory floor to his little corner office. Reaching the open door, I glance around again. None of the people in the saponification room are looking in my direction. Artem has his back turned, examining one of the stainless steel pipes.

My throat is dry as I tiptoe into the empty office. Artem's jacket is hanging on a peg just behind the door. Checking again that nobody is watching, I slide my hand into the inside pocket. My trembling fingers close on a small plastic oblong.

I draw out the device, hardly daring to believe I've been so lucky to find it already. I stare down at my palm. Now all I need—

'What the hell do you think you're doing?' Artem's voice cuts through the air.

I jump around guiltily, my fingers closing over the dongle. Artem is glaring at me from the doorway.

'What's that in your hand?' he demands.

I stare at him, my face burning.

'Show me,' Artem snaps. His eyes are fierce as lasers. His voice rises. 'Show me right now or we go straight to your grandmother.'

TWENTY-TWO

Artem holds out his hand, his beady eyes fixed on mine. '*Show* me!' he barks.

My mouth opens and shuts. I can't speak. Can't think of any way of refusing to do what he asks. Slowly, I open my hand.

Artem looks down. His eyes narrow in shock as he looks at the small black device in my palm.

He thought I'd stolen his wallet.

'Oh. What are you doing with this?' he demands.

'I just wanted to go outside for a minute,' I stammer. 'I remembered someone saying, er, that you had this . . . door sensor thing. I thought maybe I could let myself out with it.'

Artem frowns. 'So why didn't you ask to borrow it?'

I hestitate, shuffling from foot to foot. 'You, er, were busy in the saponification room. I didn't want to disturb you.' It sounds like a ridiculous, pathetic excuse, but maybe Artem will accept it.

He shakes his head then holds out his arms in disbelief.

'You can't just come into my office like this and take things without asking.'

'I . . . I'm sorry,' I stammer. 'Please don't say anything to Gran.' I offer him the sensor, thinking fast. 'I just didn't want to set off the alarm.'

'With this?' Artem holds up the device. 'This just opens the door. Nothing to do with the alarm.'

'Oh.' I make a face. 'So where is the alarm set?'

Artem shakes his head. 'It's controlled at reception. And linked up to the police station. But that's not part of your job. Now, go on – back to work.'

I hesitate. 'And you won't tell Gran?'

'No,' Artem says curtly. 'So long as you don't do any more sneaking around in people's pockets.'

'Of course,' I say. 'I promise I won't. Thank you.'

I scurry across the factory floor, back to the packaging area, where Hayley gives me a curious look.

'You were gone a long time,' she says.

'Sorry,' I say, picking up a lavender soap and placing it on the wrapping table. I busy myself fetching squares of wax paper and lilac ribbon.

We work side by side in silence. Luckily I'm used to wrapping soap by now, so my hands can operate on autopilot while my brain skitters frantically over what just happened. Will Artem tell Gran what he caught me doing, even though he said he wouldn't?

Doubt eats away at me as I place each bar of soap and fold the wrappers into position. Every time I hear footsteps I expect it to be a furious Gran, demanding to know why I've been snooping through her staff's private property.

At last the morning passes. Surely if Artem were going to tell Gran, he would have done so by now? My sense of relief lasts all of five seconds as I remember his words about the alarm system:

It's controlled at reception. And linked up to the police station.

If I don't find a way to disable the alarm first, not only will it go off as soon as the others get inside the building, but loads of police officers will then storm the place as well.

I have only a few more hours to work it all out.

Gran is out for lunch today, so Uncle Harry collects me for sandwiches at his desk. I glance at Grandad's latest motivational message:

We are the choices we make.

What does that mean? That all the good intentions in the world don't matter compared with what we actually do? I munch away at a cheese and pickle bap.

No more hesitating. It's time to act.

Next to me, Uncle Harry runs excitedly through his plans for the new Peyton Rainbow range.

'I'm thinking we should add an "all vegan" stamp to the packaging,' he says.

'Uh-huh.' I glance through to reception. As usual, Parvati is there, on the phone. I can just make out the side of her face as she runs her fingers through her hair.

'Yes, I think it will really fit with the brand,' Uncle Harry says. 'It's all coming together beautifully. We're going to start production on the first soap in days.'

'The Maya soap?' I ask.

'Exactly!' Uncle Harry claps his hands together. '*So* exciting!'

I look over at Parvati again. She finishes her call. I set down my sandwich. I'm going to ask her directly for the alarm code, even though it will definitely make me look guilty later. There isn't another option. But just as I scrape back my chair, Parvati picks up her handbag and walks to the front door. A moment later, she's gone – and with her my chance of a conversation.

'She's such a lovely person, isn't she?' Harry says with a sigh.

I turn back to him. There's a strange, almost wistful look on his face. An image of Bear suddenly shoots into my head, all tanned face and smiling green eyes. Heat rushes to my face. I'm sure Uncle Harry will see, but just then his phone rings and he turns away to answer it.

I make my way to the empty reception area and stand behind the main desk, staring at Parvati's computer. Even if I could get into it, I've no idea what to look for. I slink away, worry gnawing at my stomach. I'll have to ask about the alarm later, when she's back.

By the time Parvati returns, Harry has me sorting a load of promotional leaflets into different piles, a task which manages to be both boring and demanding. Harry himself wanders over to speak to Parvati. They're still deep in conversation when Gran pops her head around the door, announcing she's just got to make a couple of calls but will be ready to leave for home in an hour or so.

Feeling desperate, I glance over at reception again. Parvati and Uncle Harry are still talking. I can't hear what they're saying from here of course, but from the look on Parvati's flushed face, it's clearly an emotional conversation.

The copier beeps to let me know it's run out of paper. I reload the machine as I've been shown, then look up again. Parvati's on her own in reception now. There's no sign of Harry. Parvati rubs at her face. Is she *crying*?

I leave the photocopier and make my way over.

'Hiya,' I say gently.

Parvati jumps, turning to face me. Her mascara has smudged under her eyes. She wipes at it frantically. I stare at her. She's definitely been crying.

'Oh, hello, Maya. Everything okay?'

I nod. 'Um . . . are *you* all right?'

'Course,' Parvati says brightly. 'I'm absolutely fine, thank you. Just my allergies.'

'I can answer the phone for a minute, if you want to go to the bathroom?'

Parvati shoots me a grateful smile. 'Thanks, Maya,' she says. 'I won't be long.' She hurries off along the corridor.

I slip behind the cluttered reception desk. Apart from the computer, there's a big phone and an overflowing in-tray, plus a stack of folders teetering to one side. The code for the alarm has got to be written down somewhere here, hasn't it? Rummaging through the folders, I spot one with the words ALARM SYSTEM SECURITY printed on the front. I open it quickly. Page after page of bewildering text is followed by a series of diagrams. I flick through these, scanning each one as fast as I can. I stop at a picture of a numbered keypad. It looks just like the one on the control panel by the front door.

I hurry over and peer at the illuminated pad then down to the open folder in my hands. A sign on the pad says SELECT AREAS. I have a quick look around to make sure the coast is clear, then press the pad. Three squares pop up:

Factory Floor
Loading Bay
Reception/Main Entrance
INPUT CODE:

According to the instructions, this is where the alarms for the whole building can be set and deactivated. But that doesn't help me work out the code.

'You all right, Maya?' Uncle Harry materializes beside me.

I spin around to face him, feeling flustered. 'Yeah, sure, I'm great. Just wondering how this works.' I point to the control panel.

Uncle Harry shrugs. 'No idea. Parvati deals with it. She sets the alarm most nights. And if she's not around, Gran does it.' He pauses, looking around. 'Where *is* Parvati?'

'She went to the bathroom,' I say. 'Her allergies were making her eyes water.'

'Oh?' Uncle Harry hesitates, looking suddenly unsure of himself. 'So you're watching reception for her, are you? That's nice of you.' He flashes me a quick smile, then goes back to the big open-plan office.

Watching reception. Of course! I sink into the seat behind

Parvati's desk, a smile spreading across my face.

Uncle Harry's words have given me an idea.

A brilliant, super-simple idea.

At last I know exactly what I need to do.

TWENTY-THREE

I ask Parvati if I can help with the stockroom inventory that Artem said needed updating.

'That would be great!' Parvati says with a smile. Then her face falls. 'It's a very boring job, though, Maya.'

'It's fine,' I say. 'I'd like to help.'

Parvati logs me on to a spare computer in the open-plan office and I open up the stock files. I find the inventory and airdrop it to my phone, then go to the stockroom and check the list against what's actually there. Artem was right: none of the products match up. There are loads of sodium hydroxide containers, even though the computer says we are down to the last one, and just five of the big distilled water bottles, when the computer says we should have twenty.

I make a detailed list of the actual products in the stockroom, bring it back to my desk and start correcting the records. The work is as boring as Parvati said, but there's a lot of it. Which means, as I'd hoped, that when Gran comes downstairs to pick me up an hour later, I'm able to plead with her to let me stay on.

'I'm helping Parvati with the stock inventory,' I explain. 'Artem is really annoyed the data isn't accurate and I've set up a system for inputting everything, which will bring it up to date. I'd rather keep at it, especially as I left early on Monday.' I hesitate. 'Maybe Parvati could drop me off home later?'

Gran purses her lips, but I can see from the approving look in her eye that she likes my commitment. I smile to myself as she sweeps through to reception. Of course, Parvati is soon nodding, happily agreeing to leave with me later.

And so it is that at five thirty, with everyone else out of the building, Parvati announces she's locking up. I follow her out, watching carefully out of the corner of my eye as she sets the alarm using a four-number PIN followed by the hash key. I hold my breath as she presses the sequence:

3716

A sense of triumph rises inside me. *Got it.*

'How do you turn the alarm off in the morning?' I ask casually, as Parvati pulls the front door shut and locks it.

'When you open the door, it beeps and you've got thirty seconds to input the numbers before the alarm goes off and the police are called.' Parvati glances at me. 'Why d'you ask?'

'Er, Leo was wondering,' I lie, feeling instantly guilty for dragging my brother's name into it. 'You know what he's like, always wanting to understand how stuff works.'

Parvati smiles. 'He's a cute kid.' She launches into a tale about one of her nephews, apparently the same age as my brother, but I'm not listening.

I have the main entrance key and I have the alarm code. And as soon as I hand them over to CJ, Bear and Rowan tonight, CJ's plan will get underway.

The thought sends a shiver of anticipation down my spine.

I remain preoccupied all through dinner, forcing myself to follow the conversation in order to avoid Gran's sharp eyes noticing how distracted I am. Leo is telling Uncle Harry about the massive group of spider crabs he saw today and Harry is pretending to think Leo is making the whole thing up. The pre-Cornwall Leo would have got seriously wound up by this and probably burst into tears. But today he just gives an infectious giggle that makes everyone smile.

I'm the one who is wound up. My jaw aches from the

smile I have to keep faking, while inside I'm seething with anger at Gran. It's not just the terrible waste-dumping she's doing, it's the fact that she's lied to everyone about it.

The next few hours crawl by. I wait until everyone else is in bed, then tiptoe downstairs. I hurry out the back, across the lawn, through the gate and onto the beach. The route across the sand and then up to the woods is familiar to me now. Bear, Rowan and CJ are waiting when I arrive at our meeting place.

'Hi,' Bear says.

'How did you get on?' CJ asks.

I hand him the key. 'Here it is,' I say. '*And* I know the alarm code too.'

Rowan grins. 'Fantastic.'

CJ nods approvingly. 'Good work. My car is just around the corner. The container with the polluted water is already in the boot.'

A chill settles in my stomach. This is it.

A wisp of night air brushes my cheek. 'How will I get the key back?' I ask.

'We'll leave it for you under a brick by the front entrance,' CJ says. 'You can pick it up on your way in tomorrow.'

I nod. 'Good luck then.'

'Thanks, Maya,' Rowan says. 'You're a star.'

'She is indeed,' CJ adds. 'Now let's go.'

Swelling with pride, I turn to Bear, expecting to see the same impressed look on his face.

'No.' Bear shakes his head. 'No, I don't like this.'

We all stare at him.

'What?' Rowan asks, impatiently.

'Yeah, man, what's the problem?' CJ adds.

'Bear?' I touch his arm.

'We might not be breaking in, as such, but we're entering illegally and spoiling a load of their soap,' he says. 'It's too much.'

'But we aren't damaging anything,' I protest. 'Not really.'

Rowan rolls her eyes. '*Puh-lease*, Bear. You're just worried about being caught.'

'No,' Bear persists. 'It's not right. It's the kind of thing that makes people hate activists.'

'Who cares what other people think?' CJ says. 'The planet is *dying*. I'd say under those circumstances, *nothing* is too radical.'

'Exactly,' Rowan says.

But Bear shakes his head, looking stubborn.

'Maya?' he says, turning to me. 'Surely *you* can see this isn't right? You're not the kind of person who breaks the law.'

I look into his eyes. For a second I waver. Perhaps he's right. Perhaps we're going too far. Then I think about that poor baby rabbit with the broken back and it hits me again how Gran has lied and lied – and then covered up her lies – all to save money. She's put making a profit before respecting the natural world.

She has to pay for that.

'All we're doing is setting factory production back. Probably just for a day or so, while they clean out the polluted water,' I say. 'No one gets hurt.'

Bear gazes at me, his eyes filling with disappointment. 'Maya, this isn't you.'

'Don't look at me like that,' I snap, feeling instantly ashamed. 'You don't know me.'

Bear recoils, hanging his head.

'You can't back out now, man,' CJ exclaims. 'It's a three-person job: two to carry the big water bottle and one to guard the door and keep lookout.'

Bear looks up, this time avoiding my gaze. 'I won't grass you up, but I'm not doing it,' he says, his voice louder and steelier than before. 'And you guys shouldn't be either.'

'That's it then. The plan's ruined,' CJ spits. 'We can't do it without him.'

A silence falls in the darkness. I clear my throat.

'Yes, we can,' I say. 'I'll do it.'

TWENTY-FOUR

We drive in silence to the factory. I try to put Bear's disapproval – and the sad look on his face before he walked away – out of my head. CJ does most of the talking, telling us how he dropped out of uni last year because one of his tutors had it in for him. 'Kept saying I wasn't doing the work, but what was I paying student fees for then?' He shakes his head. 'The whole uni experience is such a rip-off. As soon as I started taking direct action I realized how doing this is *way* more important than a stupid degree.'

'What stuff have you done before?' Rowan asks him. She's sitting next to CJ, up front, and I'm getting the strong impression she has a massive crush on him. When we first met, I thought she was interested in Bear. But it's obvious now that she sees Bear more like a brother, that she warned me off him out of protectiveness rather than jealousy.

'Oh, loads of things,' CJ replies, swelling with pride. 'Much bigger stuff than stupid egg-throwing or people gluing themselves to buildings.'

'Yeah, I've done major stuff too,' Rowan says, but she doesn't go into any details.

'Having said that, tonight will be my biggest protest so far,' CJ goes on. There's a nasty edge to his voice that sends an uneasy shiver wriggling down my spine. I glance at Rowan, but she doesn't seem to have noticed. CJ clears his throat. 'Peyton Soaps won't know what's hit them.'

I gaze out at the passing darkness. We're almost at the factory. A sudden memory of our train journey here almost three weeks ago shoots into my head, how I'd looked out through the window and thought that life in Cornwall was going to be dull.

I couldn't have been more wrong.

CJ stops the car on the road, about a hundred metres or so from the Peyton Soaps car park entrance. 'Let's go,' he says. 'You two carry the water, so I'm free to disable the security cameras.' As we get out, CJ takes a balaclava out of his pocket and pulls it over his head, masking his entire face apart from his eyes. He looks exactly like a criminal.

My hands are sweaty with nerves as Rowan and I haul the large water container out of the boot and set it down on the tarmac. It's heavy, almost too bulky to manage between us.

'Come on!' hisses CJ, striding off towards the factory.

He's soon out of sight, lost in the dark shadows along the road.

Rowan and I heave the huge distilled water bottle up and stagger slowly after him. My arms ache with the effort.

'Did you help fill this?' I ask, peering closely at the bottle. It appears identical to all the others I saw in the stockroom. The seal looks unbroken too. Only the slight tear on the edge of the label marks it out as anything other than brand new.

'Yes,' Rowan says proudly. 'CJ spent ages resealing it so that it looked authentic. He's really inspiring, isn't he?'

'Mmm,' I say. *Really full of himself* would be more my opinion, but I don't say this to Rowan. We make our way carefully along the road. My pulse quickens as we get closer to the main building, a mixture of anxiety and excitement thrilling through my body.

CJ is waiting for us at the car park entrance. He's holding something dark and oblong-shaped in his right hand. I stare, trying to make out what it is.

'Wait here,' he says, darting forward.

Rowan and I set the water bottle down as CJ runs towards the security camera over reception. He raises his arm and, with a terrible jolt, I realize what he's holding.

A brick.

I open my mouth to shout *Stop!*, but before I can make any sound the brick smashes against the security camera above the main door, bringing the device crashing to the ground.

For a moment I stand stock-still, mouth gaping in shock. CJ gathers up the brick, then races over to the camera above the factory fire door. He's about to hurl it again.

'Stop!' I yell, running towards him. *'Wait!'*

I forget that, unlike CJ, I have no mask to conceal my face. All I can think about is the damage he's doing.

'Stop!'

TWENTY-FIVE

CJ doesn't hesitate. Before I have covered half the ground between us, he's thrown the brick. The camera over the factory fire door comes crashing down, smashing into pieces.

I skid to a stop beside him. White shards of camera casing litter the tarmac.

'What are you doing?' I demand. 'You said you wouldn't damage anything.'

CJ turns to face me. All I can see under his balaclava are his eyes, registering confusion and exasperation. 'I told you I'd take care of the CCTV,' he says. 'What did you think I was going to do?'

I stare back at him, a weird mix of shame and apprehension creeping over me. He's right, of course, but I still hate what he's done.

'Anyway,' he says with a shrug, 'the woman who runs this place can easily afford to replace a few security cameras.' He hurries across the car park to the final security cam over the loading bay. Moments later, that has crashed to the ground too, just like the others.

Rowan is still waiting with the big water bottle over by the car park gates.

'Come and help me with this, Maya!' she orders. I can hear the contempt in her voice.

I trudge over, my guts churning.

'Stop being such a loser,' Rowan hisses as I join her. 'Whose side are you on here?'

I swallow down the sick feeling in my stomach and help Rowan carry the container across the tarmac. CJ joins us by the front door, just as we're setting the bottle down. He rolls up his balaclava, revealing a frown on his narrow, fox-like face.

He glares at me. 'What was *that* about?' he demands.

I stare down at the pieces of white metal from the broken camera, scattered across the ground. Guilt rises inside me. I can just imagine how furious Gran will be, how upset Parvati will feel.

'Maya's never done anything like this before,' Rowan says with a sneer. 'She's obviously freaking out.'

CJ turns to me and places his hands gently on my shoulders. 'Only those who dare truly live,' he says.

It sounds like one of Grandad's motivational quotes.

'There wasn't a choice about the cameras,' CJ says, firmly. 'And if I hadn't smashed that second one when I did, you'd have been filmed running over to me.'

'I know,' I say.

'Good.' CJ takes his hands off my shoulders. 'Are you ready to go, Maya?'

I nod, slowly. 'I'm ready.'

'Great,' CJ says. 'Give me the key.'

Feeling numb, I hand it over.

CJ turns the key in the lock and pushes the main door open. A soft, low warning beep fills the space. CJ ushers me forwards. 'You're up, Maya,' he says. 'Quick, disable the alarm.'

My legs feel wobbly as I step over to the panel. If I don't input the code, the alarm will start blaring out in thirty seconds, bringing the police and preventing us from carrying out our plan.

'Come on,' CJ demands, his voice low in my right ear.

'Get on with it,' Rowan urges.

I take a deep breath and punch in the numbers: 3716. The low beeping stops. I stand back, as CJ and Rowan lug the water container into reception.

'Which way is the stockroom?' CJ asks, taking out his mobile and switching on the torch app.

I point towards the open-plan office. 'There's a door at the end which leads through to the factory. The stockroom's on the right-hand side in there.'

'Let's go,' Rowan says, bending down to pick up the water container again.

'Wait.' CJ grimaces. 'You keep a lookout, Rowan. Maya, you come with me. You know where we're going. It'll be faster that way.'

I open my mouth to say I'd rather wait and keep lookout, but Rowan is already saying, 'Good idea, CJ. And it'll be useful experience for Maya.'

Could she sound more patronizing?

Despite the anxiety that's building inside me, I can't help but snarl: 'Don't make out like you break into factories all the time, Rowan. *I'm* the one who stole the key and worked out the alarm code.'

Rowan shrugs. 'Whatever,' she say, giving a dismissive flick with her fingers.

'Come on, Maya.' CJ grunts as he picks up one side of the container. The torchlight from his phone peeks out from his top pocket, illuminating our way. 'Let's go.'

Shooting a final angry look at Rowan, I help CJ lift the huge water bottle, then lead him through the open-plan office to the factory. It's weird being here at night, with everywhere silent and shrouded in darkness.

'Don't worry, Maya,' CJ says, as we pass the desks in the centre of the office area. 'It's natural to freak out a bit with your first act of civil disobedience.'

He's as patronizing as Rowan! 'I wasn't freaking out,' I say, as we reach the stockroom. 'I was just worried you'd gone too far with the cameras.'

'Course you were,' CJ scoffs. He takes his phone out from his pocket. The light dances over the factory walls, creating weird, shadowy shapes. 'Like I said, first-time nerves.'

Irritated, I open the stockroom door and point towards the row of large distilled water bottles. 'Here.'

The two of us set down the container with the polluted water at the end of the row, nearest the door. CJ turns it so the torn bit of the label is hidden. 'Done,' he says proudly. 'Anyone coming in here for distilled water is automatically going to take this one.'

'Right,' I say. 'Let's go then.'

But instead of leaving, CJ strides to the back of the room. He sighs, loudly, the light from his phone flickering over the tops of the other containers. It's impossible to see their labels because they're squashed in so tightly, but I know that he's standing beside the highly flammable sodium hydroxide.

'What are you—?' I start.

'Look at all this,' he says, his voice filling with disgust. 'So much plastic. It's so wasteful: all this water used to make things we don't really need, when people around the world don't have enough to drink. The witch who runs this place is the scum of the earth.'

I bristle. It's one thing me criticizing Gran, but it hurts to hear someone else do it. Especially someone as pleased with himself as CJ.

'We don't have time for this,' I say, a sharp edge to my voice. 'Rowan will be wondering what we're doing. We need to go.'

We hurry out of the stockroom, shutting the door behind us, then race through to reception. I set the alarm again, just as I saw Parvati do earlier, then CJ locks the door behind us and gives me back the key.

He smiles. 'Well done, both of you.'

'Yeah, good job!' Rowan beams back at him. I swear she is blushing with pleasure at his praise.

I say nothing.

CJ drops me a couple of streets from Gran's house and I run the rest of the way home. Uncle Harry's key is burning a hole in my pocket so, as soon as I've let myself inside, I hurry through to his flat, using the side door in the utility room. There's no sound from his bedroom and all the lights are off. I tiptoe over to the bowl and slide the key onto the ring, then creep back to the main house.

Two minutes later I'm upstairs, safe inside Mum's old bedroom. Adrenaline still courses through me, and something else that I don't quite understand. There's no way I can sleep yet. I curl up on the window seat, staring out at the night sea. The moon shimmers over the waves.

What have I just done?

An image of the broken security cameras lying on the ground flashes into my mind. I hate that Parvati and the others at the factory will be upset at the vandalism, but Gran needed to be taught a lesson. I should feel proud of myself that I dared to be part of CJ's mission. I hug my arms around my chest. I just wish Bear hadn't seemed so against what we've done.

As I toss and turn in bed, what I'm left with is the acid fear, deep in my belly, that somehow I'll be caught – and get into real trouble. I'm going to have to appear as shocked as everyone else when the batch of soap gets spoiled.

Another lie.

As I fall asleep, it feels like I'm drowning in them.

TWENTY-SIX

A voice pulls me up, out of a deep sleep.

'Maya?' It sounds like Mum, but it can't be. Mum is hundreds of miles away, back in London. *'Maya?'*

I open my eyes.

It *is* Mum. She's sitting halfway down my bed, smiling at the shock on my face. There's a weariness about her expression but her eyes are full of love.

'Oh, Mum!' Before I even know I'm going to move, I've leaped up and into her arms. She holds me tight and I sob, suddenly realizing how much I've missed her.

'Hey, Maya,' she says, stroking my hair. 'Hey, lovely girl, what's wrong?'

The whole of last night's mission and all my feelings about it flood back.

'Nothing,' I say, pulling away and wiping my face. 'It's . . . it's just good to see you. How come you're here?'

'I missed you both.' Mum smiles. 'Plus, your gran said today is a special day, so I thought I should be here.'

Special day? I wrinkle my nose. 'What's special about it?'

197

'I'll let Gran explain.' Mum stands up. 'By the way, she says you need to get up for work.' Mum grins. 'Always was a hard taskmaster.'

'Okay,' I say, sitting up and rubbing the sleep out of my eyes.

Mum wanders over to the window and gazes out. 'This used to be my room, you know,' she says thoughtfully. 'I must have spent months curled up on that window seat when I was your age, worrying about stuff that I can't even remember now.' She indicates the crumpled cushions. 'Looks like you've been sitting here too.' She turns to me and raises her eyebrows. 'Hope you haven't been worrying like I did?'

I can't meet her gaze. 'I'd better get ready for work,' I say.

'Of course.' Mum leaves and I get dressed quickly. It's the first day since I arrived that I don't spend ages deciding what to wear in front of the mirror. I just throw on what's closest to hand. Parvati will be at the factory any minute now to open up. She'll see the broken security cameras and is bound to call Gran.

As I hurry downstairs, Gran is in the hallway. She's already on her phone. I hesitate at the bottom step.

'Thanks, Parvati. Please just get it cleared up,' she says briskly before ringing off.

'What's happened?' I ask, my heart thudding.

'Some vandals destroyed our security cameras last night.' Gran grimaces. 'At least there are no signs of a break-in, so that's something.' She clears her throat. 'Let's not worry about it for now.'

I nod, guilt and relief mingling inside me, and follow her into the kitchen. Leo is curled up on a chair right next to Mum's at the kitchen table. He spots me at the door.

'Look, Maya!' he points excitedly to Mum.

'I know,' I say, smiling in spite of my anxiety.

'I've made celebratory muffins,' Grandad says.

'Yay!' Leo cries.

'Oh, they're not for you, young man,' Grandad says, his eyes twinkling. 'I've set aside some of my ultra-healthy bran muesli for you.'

'Yuck.' Leo makes a face and everyone laughs.

Everyone except me. How long will it take before that polluted water gets mixed with lye, then with oil, and ruins production?

'Hey, sis!'

Everyone turns. Uncle Harry is in the kitchen doorway, a big smile on his face.

'Hi, Harry,' Mum says with a little less enthusiasm. She stands up and they hug briefly. The smile on Mum's face looks oddly fixed, like a mask, but I don't have time to wonder why. All I can think about is how upset everyone will be when the soap is ruined.

'Now we're all here, I think it's time for an announcement,' Gran says, as Mum and Uncle Harry sit down.

Everyone looks at her expectantly.

Gran clears her throat. 'First of all,' she says, 'I want to thank Maya for all her hard work at the factory over the past few weeks.'

'Absolutely,' says Uncle Harry.

I stare at them, feeling awkward.

'Not only has Maya helped diligently with every task assigned to her,' Gran goes on, 'she's also been instrumental in helping Harry come up with the name and design concepts for our new range, Peyton Rainbow.'

I'm blushing now, heat rising through my face. Mum beams at me.

'I'm so proud of you,' she says.

'We all are,' Gran adds crisply. 'And today marks a special day for the new range. This morning, we're putting the first Peyton Rainbow soap into production: the Maya soap.'

I stare at her, my heart sinking. I'd completely forgotten that Uncle Harry told me manufacturing was about to start.

I'm going to have ruined the very soap that's being named after me.

'Look at her,' Uncle Harry says with a chuckle, 'she's overwhelmed.'

'Aren't you excited, Maya?' Mum asks gently.

Tears prick at my eyes. I blink them away. 'Of course I am . . . it's brilliant,' I stammer.

'That's not all . . .' Gran pauses for effect. 'To celebrate your efforts, Maya, the whole family are coming to the factory this morning to see the first Maya soap bar produced.'

I stare at her, my eyes widening in panic. 'Everyone?' I gaze around the room. '*This morning?*'

Over at the kitchen table, Mum's face falls. 'Don't you like the plan, Maya?'

'It's not that,' I say. 'I . . . I'm just surprised, that's all.'

Oh no. The last thing I want is for Mum, Leo and Grandad to be present when Gran finds out that the water used for the new batch of soaps has ruined them. Anger tightens my chest. Everything I did last night and the way I'm feeling right now . . . it's all her fault.

'We'll oversee everything being set up, then watch the first few bars coming out,' Gran explains. 'And after that I'm taking everyone out for lunch.'

'Lovely,' says Mum.

'Indeed it is,' adds Grandad. 'I haven't been out for lunch with my whole family for years.'

I force a smile, though my heart feels like a dead weight in my chest. 'That's great,' I say. 'Really fantastic.'

Gran and Mum are both looking at me curiously. Mum opens her mouth, as if she's about to ask me something, but, thankfully, before she can speak, Leo starts chattering away.

'I want to see the cold press saponification machine again,' he says. 'I'll show it to you, Mum. It's really cool.'

'I'm sure it is,' Mum says, beaming at him.

Fifteen minutes later, everyone apart from me has eaten one of Grandad's muffins and we're ready to leave. Mum sits with Gran up front in her car, so I join Leo in the back. Uncle Harry is driving Grandad.

We set off, Leo still chattering away. I stare out of the window, barely listening to the conversation. After a few minutes, Mum leans across to Gran and touches her hand on the steering wheel.

'I was so worried about leaving him here, but he's a different child,' she says softly, so that Leo won't hear. 'Thank you.'

Gran shrugs. 'Nothing that a little time and attention couldn't handle. The main thing was breaking his addiction to that wretched mobile phone of his.' There's a tightness in her voice. Mum takes her hand away.

We pass the rest of the journey in silence.

When we arrive, there's no sign of any broken plastic on the tarmac. I keep my eyes averted from the wires hanging out of the wall, where the three security cameras used to be. Parvati is all smiles as we walk into reception. She and Mum greet each other like old friends. It turns out Mum was besties with Parvati's eldest sister when they were at school.

'I'm going to call the CCTV people from your office,' Uncle Harry says to Gran. 'I'll catch up with you in a few minutes.' He slips away.

'We should go through to the factory,' Gran says. 'Artem's already got a fresh batch of lye and water mixed this morning. Next step is to add the oil.'

My heart skips a beat.

'Actually, I need to speak to Artem about the updated stocklist,' Parvati says. 'I'll come with you.'

'I'll mind reception while you're gone,' I offer quickly. Anything to avoid being in the factory, knowing that the batch of soaps everyone's so excited to see is about to be ruined.

'That's kind of you, Maya.' Parvati smiles at me. 'I won't be long. Wouldn't want you to miss seeing your soaps make their entrance into the world!'

The group head off to the factory floor. Gran and Leo lead the way, while Mum holds the door open for Grandad, who hobbles through with his walking stick.

'I can't wait to see the Julies,' Mum says eagerly. 'They are still working here, aren't they?' The door swings shut behind them, muffling Grandad's reply.

Alone at last, I lean against the front of the reception desk. Outside, the sun shines with a fierce brilliance, glancing off the glass door. It feels surreal to think that I was letting myself, CJ and Rowan in through that door just a few hours ago.

Outside, a figure in a dark jacket races through the factory car park. He skids to a stop and looks up and down the building, his hand shielding his eyes from the sun's glare. I realize with horror who it is.

Bear.

What is he doing here? I fly across the room, shrinking into the shadowy wall opposite the reception desk. A moment later, Bear lowers his hand and I see a look of total fury on his face.

He starts running again, towards the front entrance.

Just a few more steps and he'll see me.

TWENTY-SEVEN

I look frantically around. The door that leads to the loading bay is just to my left. I dart through and shut it behind me. A second later, the front door buzzer sounds in reception.

What on earth is Bear doing here? And why does he look so angry? Is he planning to tell Gran that CJ, Rowan and I switched the water containers last night? Or has he somehow found out that I'm a Peyton and come to demand an explanation for my lies?

I stand for a moment in the electric light of the corridor. What I should do, I know, is go back to reception and talk to him. But I can't bear the idea of facing him right now, so, instead, I hurry along the corridor and slip inside the loading bay, where the sound of the reception buzzer can't follow me.

I shut the door quietly behind me. Sure enough, the buzzer sound disappears. It's replaced by the hiss of low, male voices, talking on the other side of the room. Hoping I can hide out until whoever they are go, I creep along the back of the loading bay. Two men – or rather the backs of their jackets – come into view. They are standing in front of the long, shuttered exit to the tarmac outside. The shutters are lowered all the way down to the ground, casting the two figures in deep shadow.

I shrink back behind a stack of boxes labelled PEYTON LIQUID SOAPS.

One of the voices rises: 'You can't just demand more money out of the blue like this.'

I blink. That's Uncle Harry. Who is he talking to? I can't see from here so, holding my breath, I edge along the metal shelving unit that runs across the back of the loading bay. I reach the final aisle. This is exactly where I found Leo hiding from the noise of the fire alarm on our first day. There's a stack of sack trucks, used for transporting big crates and boxes, just in front of me. I crouch down behind the stack. Uncle Harry is standing beside the shuttered exit. He has his back to me, but I can tell he's annoyed from the rigid way he's holding himself. The man he's talking to is mostly hidden from my view, but I can just make out a pair of grubby trainers and the bottom half of his jeans.

'But I've done all the difficult work,' Uncle Harry protests. 'Falsifying those Evo Waste receipts and uploading them onto the system. Do you think that was easy?'

My hand flies to my mouth.

'Don't you get it?' Uncle Harry goes on. 'I even bribed the Evo Waste MD to cover up for me. I took all the risk, all by myself.'

The cold truth sears into me, sending a terrible chill down my spine: Uncle Harry – not Gran – is behind the waste dumping.

'Come off it!' The man talking with Harry moves sideways, his face emerging out of the shadows at last. It's Matt Alexander, the van driver who dumped the waste that killed the poor baby rabbit.

I feel sick.

Matt jabs his finger at Uncle Harry. '*I'm* the one who keeps taking the van and offloading your stupid packaging. I risk getting caught every time I do that. And now that some bunch of eco nuts have worked out your scam, it's all getting too hot.'

I stare at the two men, horrified.

'Well, if that's your attitude I guess we're done. . .' Uncle Harry throws his hands up in frustration, then draws his wallet out of his jacket. He hands Matt Alexander a wad of banknotes. 'Clearly you don't want to make any *real* money, so take this and get out of here.'

Matt turns and thumps the mechanical door button. The long shutters grind upwards and he ducks under the metal. From here, in my crouched position, I can see his van parked just outside. He strides along the side of it, then jumps into the cab. As Matt drives away, Uncle Harry presses the mechanism again and the long, shuttered door closes.

Frightened he'll see me, I shrink back behind the sack trucks. But my shoulder knocks against the shelf beside me with a dull thud. Uncle Harry spins around.

I freeze.

TWENTY-EIGHT

I crouch further down behind the stack of sack trucks as Uncle Harry starts walking in my direction.

His phone rings, blasting into the silence.

Uncle Harry stops, snatching his mobile to his ear.

'What?' he snaps. 'Right.' He makes a face. 'Okay. Okay, I'm on my way.'

I hold my breath as he strides past my hiding place, his footsteps echoing across the loading bay's concrete floor. At last, I hear the click of the door that leads to reception closing behind him and I slump back against the shelves, letting out my breath in a shaky sigh. *Uncle Harry* has been ripping off the company all along. Dumping waste and, presumably, pocketing the money the company *should* have spent on removing and recycling it properly.

I'm too shocked even to cry. And then I remember the polluted water waiting to be mixed with lye to ruin a batch of soaps. I can't let that happen. Not now I know the waste dumping has nothing to do with Gran.

I have to warn her.

I scramble to my feet. My legs feel wobbly, my throat dry. I don't want to go back along the corridor to reception in case Uncle Harry is still there, so I stumble over to the shuttered doors and press the mechanism to open them.

With a groan and a shudder, the shutters slowly rise.

As I glance outside, Bear appears, hurrying along the tarmac. I stare at him in horror. I'd completely forgotten he was the reason I came into the loading bay in the first place.

Bear's eyes pop as he sees me, relief filling his face.

'Oh, Maya, thank goodness,' he gasps, and he races over to me. 'I've been running up and down, trying to find a way in. Listen!'

I stare at him numbly. All I can think about right now is that Uncle Harry is the Peyton Soaps criminal.

'We need to warn everyone! It's much worse than CJ said.' Bear hurries into the loading bay, grabbing my arm. 'Maya, he didn't just put polluted water in the stockroom.'

'What d'you mean?' I say.

'CJ also left a device that will start a fire,' Bear explains, eyes full of panic. 'Last night when he was here with you. Something made out of silver foil and phone batteries and . . . oh, I don't know . . . But we have to warn everyone!'

'I didn't see him leave anyth—' I stop, remembering

how CJ wandered to the containers at the back of the stockroom after we put the bottle of polluted water in position at the front.

'He was bragging to Rowan about it just now. He said this device of his would create a small fire to melt the plastic water containers and make a total mess of the stockroom which—'

'But there's not just water in there. There's oil and—' My stomach lurches.

And sodium hydroxide.

'Bear, there are chemicals stored in there. *Really flammable* chemicals!'

Bear looks at me, horrified. 'Then it won't be a small fire, it'll be a massive one. The timer's due to set it off at ten a.m.'

I whip my phone out of my pocket. 'That's in fifteen minutes!'

'Come on!' Bear tugs at my arm, trying to draw me outside the loading bay area.

'Wait!' I grab his hand. 'It'll be faster through here.'

Bear nods and, together, we race across the loading bay towards the door that leads back to reception. As we charge along the final aisle, a figure steps out of the shadows:

Uncle Harry.

I skid to a stop, Bear right beside me.

'I *knew* I'd heard someone in here.' There's no trace on Uncle Harry's face of his normal, cheerful smile. 'Where do you think you two are going?' he snarls.

'Someone's placed a device in the factory,' I say, trying to get past him. 'A device that will set off a fire. It's on a timer – about to start.'

Uncle Harry puts out his arm to stop me. 'Don't be ridiculous. It'll just be another hoax.'

'It's *true*,' Bear insists. 'We have to warn everyone.'

'And who are you?' Uncle Harry demands. There's a meanness to his voice that I've never heard before.

'He's my friend. Listen!' My voice rises to a shout, my fury bursting out of me. 'I know what you've done! And I know you don't care about anyone else in this company, but *I do*. We have to get everyone out of here before the fire starts.'

Uncle Harry tilts his head to one side. 'I don't know what you think you heard, but—'

'I heard *everything*!' I interrupt. 'The waste dumping, the stealing money, the covering it up. But none of that matters right now. We need to warn everyone about the fire.'

'People could *die*!' Bear pleads, trying to push past Uncle Harry.

To my horror, Uncle Harry grabs Bear's arm and grips it tightly. 'No, Maya,' he says. 'I'm not going to let you and your little buddy here go running to Gran, spreading lies about me.'

'They're not lies,' I shout.

'Let me go!' Bear yells.

'Get in there.' Uncle Harry turns to the cupboard right beside him and with a shove, pushes Bear inside. Bear stumbles back, falling to the ground. Uncle Harry holds out his hand to me. 'Phone, Maya. Now.'

I back away, my hand with my mobile behind my back. Uncle Harry takes a step forward and, in a single movement, wrenches the phone off me, then spins me around and pushes me into the cupboard too. I stagger into Bear, who is getting to his feet. We leap, together, to the door but, just as we reach it, it slams shut. The key turns with a click. He's locked us in!

'Hey!' Bear pounds on the door. '*Hey!*'

I drum my fists against the wood. 'Let us out!' The scream rips out of me. 'Uncle Harry, let us out!'

But the only response is the sound of the shuttered doors closing.

Then silence.

TWENTY-NINE

Bear thumps on the cupboard door. 'Help!'

I know full well that no one in the rest of the factory will be able to hear us and close my eyes, as the terrible realization settles inside me: a massive fire – which I enabled CJ to set – is about to start in the stockroom, just a few metres from my entire family.

It's all my fault. And there's nothing I can do to save the people I love.

Beside me, Bear is still hammering his fists against the cupboard door. 'Help!' he yells. 'Let us out! *Help!*'

'No one can hear,' I say dully, sinking back against the shelves to my left. The cupboard is tiny and cluttered, with cleaning materials on the shelves and a large grey bucket with a mop sticking out of it in the corner. The only light is borrowed from the loading bay and filters in through a row of tiny glass panels high above the door.

Bear stops banging on the door and turns to me, a look of bewildered shock on his face.

'You called that man "*Uncle* Harry",' he says, his voice filling with confusion.

Oh no.

He frowns. 'And before . . . he referred to "*Gran*", like . . . like she was somebody else who works here?' His eyebrows raise. 'What's going on?'

I swallow, hard, a bitter taste in my mouth. For a split second I think about coming up with a wild story to cover my tracks, but as I look into Bear's eyes I know I can't tell him another lie.

'The man who shut us in here *is* my uncle. I just found out he's responsible for the waste dumping.' I hesitate. 'And the owner, Ms Peyton, is his mother and . . . and my gran.'

Bear's jaw drops. A deep sense of shame fills me. I can't bear the hurt in his eyes.

'Why didn't you tell me?' he asks.

'Bear, I . . . it's . . .' I falter. What can I say to explain my lies? What possible reason for hiding my true identity can I give that will make any sense to him? I shake my head, still staring at the scuffed tiles on the ground.

'I'm sorry,' I mutter.

'Right.' Bear's voice tightens, his hurt morphing into anger. 'Well, we still need to warn everyone about CJ's fire. What's the time?'

215

'I don't know. Uncle Harry took my phone.' I grimace. 'But it must be almost ten.'

'Then we have to get out of here. *Now.*' He turns around and starts frantically grabbing things off the row of wooden boxes along the nearest shelf. 'There's nothing useful here,' he says. 'What about on your side?'

I see nothing but bottles of detergent and dirty rags. A messy assortment of plastic bottles and cleaning wipes are ranged across the wooden shelves. Up on the top shelf, my fingers close on a small cardboard box. I pull it down. It's full of tiny, L-shaped metal bars.

'What about these?' I shove the box at Bear. 'Could we use one to pick the lock?'

'Maybe,' he says, taking one out. 'They're Allen keys. Small ones.' He shoves the piece of metal into the door's lock, fiddles with it for a second, then turns to me. 'Is there a bigger one?'

'Not really.' I pass him the largest of the little keys.

Bear inserts it and turns.

'No use,' he snaps. 'It's still too small.' He slumps against the wall.

My pulse races, sending flickers of panic up and down my body. We have to get out of here.

'Bear?'

'What?'

'Let's break the door down.'

Bear nods. 'Come on then.' He pushes himself off the wall and points to an area right beside the lock. 'That's where the wood's weakest. Aim there.'

We line up, side by side.

'On three,' I say. 'One!'

Bear raises his leg and leans back.

'Two.' I tense my body, ready to put everything I've got into the kick.

'Three!'

With a splintering smash, the door flies open, slamming back against the wall behind. We did it!

'Where now?' Bear asks. I point to the door that leads back to reception.

'This way.' I race along the corridor, Bear at my heels. We burst into reception – the room is still empty.

'Where is everyone?' Bear demands.

'In the factory, right next to the stockroom . . .' My voice breaks at the thought of Mum and Leo and Gran and Grandad being there, with no idea of what's about to hit them. 'Come on!' I cry.

I'm about to run off, when my eye lights on the fire alarm panel on the wall. My fist hovers over the glass.

'Do it!' Bear urges.

I smash the alarm. A piercing screech blares out. We

run on, side by side, through the empty open-plan office and into the factory. I skid to a halt just inside, trying to work out where my family are. The factory floor is full of people shouting over the screaming alarm as they stream out of the building through the fire door. Across the room, I spot Gran. She's standing outside the saponification area, gesticulating wildly at Artem, while Parvati ushers Grandad through the exit.

Artem moves sideways and I see Mum. Leo's there too, his hands over his ears as the alarm screeches. I glance over at the stockroom, just a few metres from where they're standing.

I take a step towards Mum and Leo.

At that moment, Leo breaks away from her, hands still over his ears.

I freeze. He's making for the stockroom, to get away from the noise—

'*Stop!*' I yell, but my voice comes out hoarse. Unheard.

In a single, swift movement Artem turns. He grabs Leo, spinning him around.

And then time seems to slow down as, just a few metres beyond them, a ball of fire explodes through the stockroom door.

Roaring like thunder, it rolls and leaps up to the ceiling, obliterating everything.

THIRTY

I'm too shocked even to scream as the fireball flares up, up, to the ceiling, then recedes, leaving spirals of flame licking along the room as far as the outer walls of the saponification area. Thick, grey smoke pours out of the space where the stockroom door used to be.

Panic spirals inside me. I clutch Bear's arm as I strain my eyes to see through the smoke. Where are Mum and Gran?

Where is Leo?

As I look desperately around, the smoke thins. Gran and Mum emerge through the gloom. Neither have noticed me. Mum clutches her hair. 'Leo!' she screams.

'Everyone out!' Gran's voice rises above the alarm that's screeching above the emergency exit door. '*Now!*'

'Leo!' Mum shouts again.

Heart in my mouth, I turn towards the spot on the floor where I last saw my brother, being spun away from the stockroom by Artem.

Artem is still there, waving his arms at Mum. 'Get

back!' he shouts, running towards her. 'Get back!'

'Where's Leo?' Mum's shriek rises above everything else. Instead of running away, she starts racing towards the smoke.

'No!' My voice is hoarse.

Bear catches my arm. 'Maya! We need to get out of here!'

Across the room, Artem reaches Mum. He lifts her off the floor. She's kicking at him, but he's too strong.

'Leo isn't in here!' Artem shouts. 'He tore out of my arms straight after the explosion. He must be outside already. *Come on!*'

Mum stops struggling and Artem sets her down. Together, they race towards the emergency exit, joining Gran on the way. They still haven't seen me and Bear across the room.

The smoke curls around our feet. It stinks of grease and chemicals.

'Maya!' Bear shouts again, tugging on my arm. 'We need to get out too!'

I pull back. 'No,' I cry. 'I have to find my brother. I have to find Leo.'

'That man said he was outside.' Bear's eyes widen. 'Maya, *please!*'

'No!' I shake my head, stubbornly. 'Leo hates noise.

He'd have tried to get away from the alarm.'

Like he did the first time it went off . . .

'I know where he's gone!' I race out of the factory and into the empty office. Over the alarm, I hear Bear behind me, slamming shut the door. I dart past all the desks, then fly through reception and along the corridor that leads to the loading bay. Down here, the sound of the alarm is already muffled. I tear into the loading bay, almost tripping over the same cupboard door that Bear and I kicked open just minutes earlier.

'Maya!' Bear yells, still behind me. 'Where are we going?'

I pound down the first aisle. 'Leo?' I shout. *'Leo!'*

I run along the front of the loading bay, glancing up each aisle as I pass. No sign of him . . . I turn, panting, into the final aisle and skid to a stop. I'm so sure Leo will be here, crouching on the ground with his hands over his ears, just like he was the last time.

But as I stare wildly at the scuffed concrete floor and the metal shelves in front of me, I realize that I'm wrong.

Leo is nowhere to be seen.

THIRTY-ONE

I stare around the loading bay, all my breath knocked away. Waves of terror crash over me.

Where is Leo?

'Maya!' Bear gasps, panting for breath. I turn to face him. 'What are we doing in here?'

'I . . . I thought Leo would be here,' I stammer. 'He hid here once before when . . .' I trail off, desperately trying to work out where else Leo might have gone.

Bear studies me for a second. 'So when you said you had a little brother, that wasn't a lie then?'

I shake my head, shame piercing my fear, then turn away from him.

'I have to check Gran's office. It's the quietest room in the factory.'

'Why not let the fire brigade do that?' Bear suggests.

I stare at him. 'Do you hear any sirens?'

'Not yet,' Bear concedes, 'but they must be on their—'

'I'm not waiting.' I run back through the loading bay and along the corridor. It's my fault that Leo is in danger.

If I'd been honest with everyone from the start, then none of this would be happening.

As I tear through reception, I realize Bear is still following me. 'Go outside!' I shout, pointing to the main entrance, before darting away, through to the big open-plan office again. Tendrils of smoke are already curling under the door to the factory floor, the alarm still shrieking away.

'Which way?' Bear has ignored my request to leave. I don't have time to argue with him. We race up the stairs, our footsteps springing lightly on the steps.

Tearing into Gran's office, there's still no sign of Leo. Where *is* he?

'Look!' Bear yells, pointing at Gran's desk.

In two steps I'm there. Leo is huddled beneath the desk, hands firmly clamped over his ears. A sob of furious relief wells up inside me. I crouch down beside him and take his arm as gently as I can.

'Hey, Leo.'

My brother looks up at me, fear in his eyes.

'Too noisy,' he says.

'I know.' I ease him out from under the desk and hug him tight.

'We need to go,' Bear urges. I nod.

'Come on, Leo,' I say, trying to keep my voice calm.

Holding my brother's hand, I follow Bear to the door that leads down to the open-plan office.

'Oh no!' Bear cries.

I push past him, to the head of the stairs. My heart skips a beat. The fire has already spread across the area between the stairs and the factory door. Its fingers clutch at the desks and chairs; its tongues lick the bottom steps, directly beneath us.

Beside me, Leo gasps. 'What do we do, Maya?'

I grip his hand more tightly, my mouth still hanging open. I turn to Bear. I'm sure he can read the question in my eyes. He shakes his head. We both turn our gaze back to the stairs beneath us.

The fire is already jumping up, faster than seems possible. Fresh flames are burning halfway up now.

There's no way out.

THIRTY-TWO

I stare at the fire, transfixed by the crackling flames as they leap and curl up the stairs. The insistent shriek of the alarm pulses in my head. A cloud of dark grey smoke billows towards us—

'Maya!' Bear's voice brings me back to the present. He tugs at my arm, pulling me back into Gran's office. We stumble inside and slam the door shut behind us. Leo immediately scuttles over to Gran's desk and dives underneath it again.

'What are we going to do?' Bear asks, desperation in his eyes. 'Nobody even knows we're here.'

I hurry over to the desk and pick up the phone. Silence.

'The line's dead,' I say.

'The window!' Bear races to the high glass at the end of the room.

I follow, hoping that somehow the distance to the ground will have miraculously shortened, but of course the drop is as long and severe as ever.

'We can't.' Bear's voice fills with despair. 'There's not

even a ledge to crawl out onto.'

I glance at Leo, still squeezed under Gran's desk. The first wisps of smoke are curling up from underneath the door.

It's my fault we're trapped in here.

My fault that the factory is on fire.

My fault that the three of us are almost certainly going to die.

'Can't we get out through that?' Bear points to the skylight set into the sloping roof above the desk.

'Let's try,' I say. 'Even if we can't get down to the ground from there, we'll be further away from the smoke.'

As Bear shoves the computer to one side, I scramble on top of the desk and push the slanted window up and open. The sky above is full of clouds and a gust of wind whips across my face as I put my arms out over either side of the frame. I haul myself up, then wriggle through. Out on the roof I catch my breath, crouching low against the incline of the tiles. I'm on a short, steep slope overlooking the front of the building. Looking down, all I can see from here is a narrow strip of car park and the gates beyond it. I spot the two Julies and Hayley standing on the tarmac. I can tell from the way they're hugging their arms around their chests that they're terrified. Shame fills me again.

'Hey!' I yell. 'Hey! Up here!' But my words are whisked away on the breeze.

I catch a whiff of burnt plastic and turn. To my horror, the vents from the saponification room are pumping out thick clouds of grey smoke. At the moment, the wind is blowing them towards the distant trees, but if it changes direction, we'll be smothered.

'Maya?' Bear urges. 'Is there a way down?'

'No!' I duck my head back inside. A steady stream of smoke is now curling under the door. 'We can't get off the roof from up here – it's too high,' I explain, 'but if we all shout, maybe they'll see us.'

'Got it. Come on, Leo.' Bear helps my brother onto the desk, then picks him up and guides him through the skylight.

'Maya!' Leo squeals.

'It's okay,' I say, yanking Leo by the armpits and easing him onto the sloping roof. 'Just stay close to the tiles.'

Leo is wide-eyed as he shuffles sideways. 'This is very high up,' he says uncertainly. 'We must be nearly five metres off the ground.' He gulps. 'At this height, there's a strong chance of being badly hurt if we jump. Though the median distance for lethal falls is fourteen metres, so we probably wouldn't be killed.'

'Reassuring,' Bear mutters.

'Please stay still, Leo,' I say.

Leo obediently huddles against the tiles, as Bear now eases himself out through the opening. He crouches down, holding onto the side of the skylight as he leans out, scarily far from the roof. Hayley is still visible by the car park gates.

'Hey!' Bear shouts, waving his free arm. 'HEY!'

She doesn't look up.

I grip the side of the skylight with one hand, like Bear has done, and take Leo's arm with the other. 'Come on,' I urge him. 'Let's yell together. One . . . two . . .'

'HEY!!!' The three of us shout together. 'UP HERE!'

Hayley still doesn't hear. A moment later she drifts out of sight.

A siren sounds faintly in the distance.

'Is that the fire brigade?' I cry.

'It must be,' Leo says shakily. 'Standard response times are less than nine minutes and the alarm started at least seven minutes ago.'

I glance at Bear, hope filling me for the first time. Once the firefighters get here, they will rescue us. And surely they'll be here in just a few minutes.

But Bear is staring, horrified, at the billowing smoke behind us. A second later, the wind changes direction. A cloud of acrid, toxic smoke blasts across our faces, making us cough. Bear meets my gaze. I can see the awful truth in his eyes: we might not have a few minutes.

'Let's try shouting again!' I cry.

Bear nods.

'Come on, Leo. One. Two . . . *HELP!*'

The three of us let out ear-splitting yells.

I peer over the edge. The ground is dizzyingly far away. A woman is hurrying across the tarmac. She reaches the gates just as a fire engine roars into view.

'It's Mum!' I cry, leaning out further. '*Mum!*'

'Is she there?' Leo wriggles forwards. Too far forwards. With a terrified yelp, he slips down the slope. Still gripping his arm, I tumble after him, bumping over the hot, rough tiles.

There's no time to scream. All I know is that I can't let go of Leo.

I can't let him fall.

Time slows down, as the edge of the roof hurtles towards me.

THIRTY-THREE

Bear grabs my ankle. With a jerk, I stop falling. I'm at full stretch along the rough slant of the short, steep roof. My head is pointing down towards the ground. Beneath me, Leo is dangling, his legs beyond the edge of the tiles. A thin scream of terror escapes from his mouth.

I twist my neck, looking back up the roof. Bear is clutching the side of the skylight with one hand. The other is around my foot.

Only Bear's hold is keeping me from falling.

Only my grip on Leo's arm is stopping his fall.

I want to shout for help again. But I can't find my voice. All my energy is in the hand holding tightly to Leo's arm. I'm hanging on as hard as I can, but I can feel my fingers tiring, my grip starting to loosen.

As the smoke around us is whipped away, I close my stinging eyes.

Please. I can't lose my brother. Not like this.

'Maya!' Suddenly I'm aware that an unfamiliar voice is calling out to me. 'You can let go of Leo now.'

As my eyes spring open, I realize that my brother's body weight is no longer pulling at my hands. A firefighter is staring up at me. She's holding Leo, his arms wrapped around her neck. They're inside a ladder platform box extended from the fire engine below.

'My name's Siân,' the firefighter says. 'Let Leo go, he's safe.'

I release my grip on my brother's arm. Siân sets him down inside the box, then shouts something I can't hear to the people below. The ladder extension clanks as the platform box rises.

'Now you.' Siân gathers me under the shoulders. She glances up, presumably at Bear, and nods. I feel Bear's hand release my ankle and I sink into the firefighter's arms. She eases me onto the platform floor, then shouts something up to Bear. As I collapse against the side of the box, Leo huddles against me, his eyes squeezed tight shut.

I glance down to the ground. Mum is peering anxiously up at us, her hands over her mouth. Beside her, Gran is saying something, her own hand resting on Mum's shoulder.

A second later, Bear is leaping smoothly into the box. He gasps for breath, massaging his wrist, as we're lowered to the ground. As soon as we stop moving, Siân opens a hatch in the side of the box and Leo races out, straight into Mum's arms. She staggers backwards, keeping one arm outstretched for me. I fall against her, letting myself be half dragged, half carried across the tarmac. Smoke hovers around us for a moment, then we're through, past the gates, to where an ambulance is waiting.

Mum ushers me and Leo towards the nearest paramedic – a middle-aged man with a deep crease in his forehead. Suddenly we're inside the ambulance, the man examining us, asking questions about the fire and the smoke. How close we were, how much we inhaled.

'Hardly any,' I say truthfully.

'We still need to get you properly checked out at hospital.' The paramedic looks at Mum.

She nods. 'I'll ride with you.'

'Wait, what about Bear?' I ask. 'Did he get out okay?'

'The boy who saved you?' Mum asks. 'He's over there.'

I glance across the tarmac. Bear is visible through the back of another ambulance. He's lying down. A paramedic is leaning over him. I can't see his face.

'Is he okay?' I ask. I try to push myself up, to get out of the ambulance. I need to find out if Bear is all right.

But just then the back doors slam shut and I'm jolted back down onto the trolley. A second later, the engine starts and we drive away.

THIRTY-FOUR

I've been at the hospital for what seems like ages and I still haven't seen Bear. Once it's clear that Leo and I are basically fine, we're put in a waiting area with Mum. The nurses say they'd like us to stay here for a few hours so that they can monitor us a bit longer, then a doctor will give us a final check and we'll be able to go home.

Another half-hour passes and Gran and Parvati arrive. I keep hoping Bear will walk in, but there's no sign of him. Mum sits in the corner of the room, Leo on her lap. He doesn't usually like lots of hugging, but today he's content to lie against her as she strokes his arm. She's already asked me if I know who Bear is and what he was doing at the factory. So far I've sidestepped her questions, simply saying that, by turning up when he did, he saved all our lives.

I know I need to explain more. I need to tell Mum – and Gran – why Bear came to the factory this morning. But that means telling them about CJ and how he deliberately set the fire. Which will also mean telling them about my part in his original plan – and about Uncle Harry's terrible betrayal.

And I haven't found the words to do any of that yet.

Gran paces up and down, as tense as Mum is calm. Parvati trots along by her side, running through a list of staff.

'Nobody is injured,' Parvati says breathlessly. 'And everyone's accounted for, except . . .' She hesitates.

'Who?' Gran demands. '*Who* isn't accounted for?'

'Er, Harry,' Parvati says, reluctantly. 'He was seen driving away from the factory just after the alarm sounded, but I can't get hold of him now.'

'I've left messages as well,' Gran says. 'Where on earth has he got to?'

'At least we know he wasn't caught up in the fire,' Parvati reassures her.

'And Dad should be back home by now,' Mum adds, 'so he can call us if Harry shows up there.'

'I'm sure there's no need to worry,' Parvati says.

Gran blows out her breath. 'Let's hope so.'

I glance at Mum. She's gazing up at Gran, deep concern etched on her face.

Guilt twists inside me again.

'They've managed to put out the fire,' Parvati goes on. 'They're already trying to work out how it started.'

I fidget, suddenly uncomfortable in my seat.

'Someone must have accidentally decanted lye into an aluminium container; that could start a fire.' Gran sighs, then walks over to the window at the end of the room. 'It's the only explanation I can think of.'

'I can't imagine Artem or his team making a mistake like that,' Parvati says, frowning.

'I suppose not.' Gran clutches the windowsill and peers out.

Even from where I'm sitting, I can see her knuckles are white with tension.

'Although . . .' Parvati twists her hands together, her voice cracking with emotion. 'Artem had been saying for days that the stockroom was a mess. If only I'd got it sorted sooner . . .' she trails off.

'Gran?' I stand up.

I need to come clean. Right now. Before I get too terrified to do it.

Gran turns. 'Yes, dear?'

But before I can continue, the waiting-room door opens and Drina, Bear's mum and Rowan walk in. My stomach lurches into my throat.

Bear's mum sees me straight away. 'Oh, Maya,' she says. 'Are you all right?'

'I'm fine.' I hurry towards her. 'How about Bear?'

'He's fine. Getting some air outside.' Bear's mum's mouth trembles a little. 'He just sprained his wrist. He's had a X-ray. No bones broken.' She turns to Drina, who puts an arm around her shoulders.

From the way they're talking, I'm guessing that Bear hasn't told them who I really am. I'm suddenly aware that Mum is watching us from her chair and that Gran and Parvati have stopped their conversation to stare at us too.

A wave of foreboding washes over me.

'Rowan told us about CJ,' Drina says, beckoning Rowan over from where she's standing by the door. 'We called the police straight away.'

Rowan walks over. Her eyes are red-rimmed; she's obviously been crying hard. She looks up. 'I can't believe CJ lied to us,' she says. 'I can't believe what . . . what he did.' A tear trickles down her cheek.

I glance over at Gran. She's listening intently.

Before I can respond, Rowan's arms slide around me. She squeezes me tight. 'I didn't tell them that you were with me and CJ,' she breathes in my ear. 'Neither did Bear. They don't know you were involved at all.'

My heart skips a beat. 'Thank you,' I whisper back.

Rowan releases me, smiling, then says, more loudly: 'I'm so glad you're okay, Maya.'

Across the room, Mum stands up. Parvati takes her

place beside Leo, as Mum and Gran walk towards us.

'Hello,' Gran says. 'I gather from what you've said that you're here with the boy who helped Maya and Leo. We're very grateful to him. Bear, is it?'

Drina nods. She holds out her hand. 'Drina Dragone,' she says. 'And this is Bear's mum, Val.'

Gran introduces herself and they all shake hands. Gran's brows knit. 'I feel I know you from somewhere,' she says.

'You do.' Drina makes a wry face. 'We're from the Harmony Earth Group.'

'Ah,' says Gran. 'Yes, well . . .'

'How do you know Maya?' Mum asks, moving closer.

I stare around the circle of faces: Mum . . . Bear's mum and Drina . . . Rowan . . . Gran . . . It's my last chance to speak out, before my lies swallow me up for good.

But the words won't come. Instead, I'm left staring helplessly at Bear's mum as she smiles gently and says: 'Maya, Bear and Rowan became friends a few weeks ago. She's been to our community lots of times. She told us about her summer job with your company.'

Gran blinks, a look of confusion on her face. 'Maya's been to your camp?' She looks at me.

I stare at my toes.

Drina nods. 'We'd like to call Maya's mum, if you haven't already, to let her know she's okay. If she's heard the news about the fire, the poor woman will be worried sick.'

'And that won't help with her condition,' Bear's mum adds.

'Her *condition*?' Mum's voice fills with bewilderment.

I close my eyes.

'Yes,' Drina continues. 'Maya told us all about it: how her mum's barely mobile, how Maya is her principal carer—'

'*What?*' Gran's own voice rises.

'Maya?' Mum's voice, right beside me, is flat with shock. She puts her hand on my arm. 'Maya, what on earth?'

I open my eyes. Everyone is looking at me.

'Excuse me,' Drina says to Mum, concern in her eyes. 'But who exactly are you?'

'I,' says Mum, drawing herself up, '*I* am Maya's mother.'

Drina and Bear's mum stare at her. I wish for time travel, an earthquake, a miracle.

Instead:

'And I'm her grandmother,' Gran adds, icily.

'Whoa!' Rowan gasps.

'Well, Maya?' Mum's voice is tight with confusion and anger. 'I think you have some explaining to do.'

I open my mouth and gaze at the faces around me. I've lied to all of them.

And there's nothing I can say that they'll understand.

No way that any of them will ever forgive me.

Without a word, I run out of the waiting room.

THIRTY-FIVE

I find Bear near the main entrance, sitting on a bench by a flower bed of fading roses. His left wrist is bandaged and resting in a sling. He's leaning back, eyes closed, face tipped to the sky. The sun filters through the leaves on the tree above the bench, glancing off his blond hair – just like it did the first time I saw him at the edge of Penwillick Wood.

I need to apologize to him properly. I owe him that at the very least. I take a small step forwards. I barely make a sound but, somehow, Bear hears. His eyes open and he turns his head towards me. He stiffens, his expression instantly wary.

'Hello,' I say, suddenly feeling awkward.

'Hi.' He looks away, towards the flowers.

I perch on the bench beside him, twisting my fingers together. 'Is your wrist okay?'

'It's fine. Just a sprain.' He's still not looking at me.

'I saw your mum and Drina upstairs. And Rowan. They just met Gran . . . and my mum.'

'Oh.' Bear meets my gaze at last. His voice is dry and ironic. 'How did *that* go?'

I grimace. 'It all came out. How I've been visiting your camp, how I'm a . . . a Peyton.' Bear stares, evenly, at me. He says nothing. 'I . . . I . . . couldn't handle it . . . I ran away.'

'Of course you did,' Bear says, and his sour tone makes my heart sink.

'I ran away because I wanted to find you,' I say quickly. 'To apologize for lying and to thank you for . . . for saving me and Leo.'

Bear gives a swift nod.

'Also, I . . . I wanted to thank you for not telling everyone how I helped CJ get inside the factory. Rowan explained they don't know I was involved and I can't tell you what a relief that is. I mean, things are bad en—'

'You should thank Rowan for that,' Bear interrupts. 'She insisted we shouldn't give you away. She was worried about you getting the sack.' He gives a mirthless laugh. 'As if *that* was going to happen, when your family run the place.'

I stare at him. I've never heard him sound sarcastic before.

'I haven't told anyone, not even Rowan, who you really are,' Bear goes on. 'I thought I'd give you the chance to do that yourself.'

His words hang in the air. I decide to divert the conversation away from me.

'When did Rowan find out what CJ was planning?' I ask.

'This morning. She went to his hut and found him packed and ready to leave, so she went with him to his car, which was parked a mile or so out of camp. Apparently he couldn't help boasting about what he'd *really* done.' Bear shakes his head, clearly disgusted. 'It turns out CJ has had it in for the factory ever since he arrived. He made the hoax bomb call that the police thought we were behind.'

I gasp. 'That was CJ? *Why?* The bomb scare happened *before* we found out about the waste being dumped.'

'Mum reckons he was looking for something to get upset over. She says people like him always are.' He shrugs. 'Anyway, CJ drove off and Ro started running back to camp. She saw me on the way, told me about the fire starter he'd planted. I ran to the factory to warn everyone.' He meets my gaze, intense hurt blazing in his eyes. 'I mostly just wanted to make sure you were safe.'

'I'm so sorry,' I blurt out.

Bear raises his eyebrows. 'For what? You didn't know what CJ was really planning any more than me or Rowan.'

'Not that . . . I'm sorry for lying, for not telling you who I really was. I just . . . I thought that if you knew I

242

was a Peyton you wouldn't want anything to do with me.'

'Why would you think that?' Bear frowns.

'From how angry everyone was about Gran doing that appeal against your camp.' I bite my lip. 'And . . . and because some people said you were a violent group, so I didn't know what you might do if . . .' I trail off.

Bear stares at me. 'How ironic,' he says. 'You had *no proof* that we would do anything that might hurt anyone, yet you ended up helping someone set a fire that could have killed an entire factory full of people.'

'I . . . I know,' I stammer.

'Well, you've achieved one thing: any local person that *didn't* think we were violent before, will certainly think that now.'

I stare at him. 'I hadn't thought of that.'

'No,' he says. 'Not thinking about stuff seems to be your thing, doesn't it?' He shifts slightly, turning away from me.

'Please, Bear.' I edge closer to him, my eyes pricking with tears.

Bear says nothing, just stares at the roses.

'I can see how angry you are,' I say, a lump in my throat. 'My gran and my mum are mad at me too. And I understand. I know I shouldn't have lied, but it was impossible to . . . to . . .'

'To what? Be honest?' Bear meets my gaze, a hardness in those pale-green eyes. 'You still don't get it, do you?'

'Get what?' My voice breaks.

'When I met you, I thought you were really cool, but you're just spoilt and selfish.'

'What?' I stare at him, bewildered. 'What do you mean?'

'You could have just *asked* what the truth was.' Bear's voice fills with emotion. 'Even if you'd heard a load of rumours, you could see how we lived, how peaceful we—'

'I know. I *did* ask.'

'But instead of believing us and trusting what your own eyes told you, you made up a story about your mum being ill and you having to care for her.' Bear's voice rises angrily. 'You did all that so you'd look like a victim, to make out like you're this loving, selfless daughter.' He snorts. 'The only person you love is yourself.'

Pain rises through my chest, filling my whole body.

'That's not true.' The words come out as a whisper, half strangled. 'Bear?'

But Bear isn't listening. He has already turned and is walking away.

THIRTY-SIX

I stare down at my lap, the grubby grey of my joggers blurring as tears fill my eyes. Around the bench there are small noises: the distant murmur of conversation, the low hum of traffic from the road beyond, the rustle of the leaves overhead.

Bear's so wrong about me. That is, he's right that I lied and it's understandable that he's angry, but I was only dishonest with people to avoid hurting them. I didn't want Bear and the eco camp to think I hated them like the rest of my family seemed to. And I didn't tell Gran about my visits to the camp because I didn't want to upset her.

Why can't he see that?

Over at the hospital entrance, two nurses are chatting as they look at something on a phone. An old man sits hunched over on a bench beside them, smoking a cigarette. I bury my face in my hands, a tear trickling through my fingers.

Footsteps sound on the path beside me.

I look up, eagerly. But it's not Bear standing in front of me.

It's Uncle Harry.

I jump up off the bench, startled.

'Hi, there, Maya. Thank goodness you're all right.' He's trying to give me that cheery smile of his, but I can see the strain in his eyes and the tightness of his jaw.

I clench my fists, anger rising in my chest. 'What do you want?'

Uncle Harry opens his arms wide, a gesture of peace, of surrender. 'Maya, *please*, I came to give you your phone back.' He hands me my mobile. 'I'm sorry about shutting you and your friend in that cupboard. I panicked and—'

'We told you about the fire and you left us in a *locked*—'

'Okay, okay,' he admits, 'but in my wildest dreams I never thought . . .' He sighs. 'Come on, Maya, the whole thing sounded like another hoax.'

I stand, silent, staring at my phone.

'Anyway, I *didn't* leave,' Uncle Harry goes on. 'I was just trying to buy some time.' He pauses, turning away from me and running his fingers through his fringe, as if collecting his thoughts.

An idea strikes me. I quietly tap on my phone and glance up at him.

'So what *did* you do?' I ask. 'After you shut us in the cupboard?'

Uncle Harry turns and gazes at me, an earnest, pleading

expression in his eyes. 'Okay, I'll be honest. The first thing I thought about was undoing the changes I'd made to the company records . . .'

'You mean deleting the evidence that you invented receipts and stole money?'

'Yes, but . . .' A pained look crosses Uncle Harry's face. 'I quickly realized nothing I could do would be enough, so I decided to pack up my stuff and get as far away as possible.'

'To run away?' I sneer, then stop. Isn't running away – from Mum and Gran and all the others in the hospital waiting room – exactly what *I've* just done?

'I was getting into my car,' Uncle Harry goes on, ignoring me, 'when the fire alarm sounded, so I came back. I *swear* I did. I went to the loading bay and found the cupboard door kicked down, so I knew you'd already got out. I went outside and I could see your mum and gran. I assumed you were with them and . . . and I left again.' He screws up his face. 'As soon as I heard the news, that some kids had been rescued from the factory fire and were in hospital, I turned right around and came here to make sure you were all right. Of *course* I did. You're my family . . .' He hesitates. 'Your gran has been messaging me, asking where I am, so I know you haven't told her about me yet.'

I stare at him.

'No matter what you think, Maya, I'm not a bad person.'

'Oh, right,' I snap. 'Just a greedy one.'

Uncle Harry flinches. 'Maya, that's not fair—'

'I'd say defrauding your family's company and dumping waste that pollutes the countryside in order to have more money for yourself makes you *exactly* a greedy person. Don't you think?'

'No.' Uncle Harry frowns. 'No, you don't understand. I . . . I *need* that money. I got into massive debt buying my car; my salary doesn't even cover the repayments.' He pauses. 'Don't you see? I had to get hold of more cash, and I wasn't hurting anyone by siphoning a bit off the company. All I did was cut a few corners; it isn't that big a deal.'

I shake my head at how self-pitying he sounds and take a step away, but Uncle Harry moves sideways, blocking my path.

'I only lied about what I did to avoid upsetting your gran,' he says. 'I was *protecting* her. I *love* her.'

'Yeah, right.' I stare at him. 'The only person you love is yourself.'

With a jolt, I realize those are the same words Bear used about me a few minutes ago. Worse, Uncle Harry's excuse about not wanting to upset Gran by being honest is exactly how *I* justified keeping quiet.

The truth is that I did have a choice. I could have been honest. But instead I've lied to everyone I love.

And the consquences almost killed my entire family.

'You've got this all wrong, Maya,' Uncle Harry persists. 'I—'

'I don't want to hear any more,' I interrupt. 'If you didn't like working for Gran, you should have left. Not stolen from her. I'm going to tell her what you've done. Right now.' I try to move past him again, but Uncle Harry puts out his arm to stop me.

'Wait.' He grabs my arm. I wrench it away from him. 'Please, just listen, Maya. I want to make a deal with you.'

'A deal?' I look into his hazel eyes, so like Mum's in colour, yet without any of Mum's kindness or patience.

'Don't tell your gran what I did,' Uncle Harry says, 'and I'll give you a monthly allowance for clothes and whatever else you want, for the rest of the time you're at school, maybe even at uni.'

I look deep into his panic-stricken eyes. 'Are you serious?'

'Yes.' Harry sucks in his breath. 'There's no need to tell your gran that I took money from the company. All the records will have been destroyed in the fire. You're the only person who knows I faked those receipts and kept the money for myself. If you keep quiet, then I can help your gran rebuild the business.'

'But—'

'Think how upset she'll be if she knows what I've done. I won't be able to carry on working with her and she'll be *devastated*.'

For the first time, I hesitate. Gran adores Uncle Harry, she always has. Learning of his betrayal will cut her to the core. But . . .

'She deserves to know the truth,' I say stubbornly.

'Why?' Harry demands. 'What good will it do? Your gran will be absolutely on her knees over having to rebuild the factory. The last thing she needs is a massive emotional upset on top *and* to lose her most important member of staff.'

'I'd say Parvati or Artem are more important to Peyton Soaps than you.'

Uncle Harry shrugs. 'Whatever. The point is that I matter the most to your gran. You *know* I do—'

'Maya! Harry!'

We turn towards the voices across the grass. Mum and Gran are hurrying towards us, Parvati at their side.

'Maya, please,' Harry says, his voice urgent. 'I'll pay you two hundred pounds a month to keep your mouth shut. Imagine all the outfits you could buy with that kind of money.'

I meet his gaze.

Mum reaches me first. 'Why did you run off, Maya?' she says, her voice thick with emotion.

Beside us, Gran embraces Uncle Harry. Next to them, Parvati watches on. A strange expression passes over her face: relief, for sure. But something else, too; something I can't read.

Gran releases Harry. 'I've been calling and calling you, son,' she says.

'I know,' Uncle Harry says, 'I'm sorry. I was in a bit of a state over the fire.' He throws me a meaningful look. 'But I'm over that now. And I'm here, ready to help by doing whatever I can.'

'Thank you,' Gran says shakily. 'This is just awful, isn't it? But at least they know who's responsible.'

'One of those eco nutters, was it?' Uncle Harry asks.

'Actually a *visitor* to their camp,' Mum cuts in. 'The people who run it had no idea.'

'That's right,' Gran adds. 'An activist called CJ. He's the one responsible for the bomb scare too.'

'And the eco nuts told you all this?' Uncle Harry sounds deeply sceptical.

'Don't call them that,' Mum says. 'Drina – she runs the place – she and her partner are devastated by what this CJ did. They called the police as soon as they found out.'

'Their son, Bear, who Maya knows, even ran over to the factory,' Gran goes on. 'He sounded the alarm. Saved everybody without a single thought for his own safety.'

'Including Maya and Leo,' Mum adds.

'Okay, well I guess that's something.' Uncle Harry shoots me another look. 'So how much damage is there? Will the insurance cover it?'

'I think so,' Gran says. 'But we won't be operational for at least three months, so—'

'Gran,' I say.

She looks at me. 'What is it, Maya?'

I can feel Uncle Harry's eyes on my face, burning my skin.

'I . . . I'm sorry I lied about meeting up with Bear and the others. You were just so anti the camp, I thought you'd stop me from seeing them.'

Gran's face falls. 'I understand. I mean, I wish you hadn't felt the need to lie, but I can see why you did. I'm actually starting to think I may have been wrong about them. At least, I was wrong about Drina and her partner. They're just trying to live in a different way, but there's no violence in them.'

'You shouldn't have told them such an awful lie about me though, Maya,' Mum adds quietly.

'I know,' I say, hanging my head. Mum sighs and hugs

me. I catch Uncle Harry's eye. He's watching me carefully. Parvati is looking at me too, though – again – I can't read her expression.

I'm standing at a crossroads.

I can tell the truth: that I let CJ into the factory because I thought Gran was responsible for illegally dumping waste, when in fact that was Uncle Harry.

Or I can keep quiet.

Bear and Rowan have kept me out of the factory break-in and, even if CJ tells the police I was there, it will just look like he's trying to shift the blame from himself. As for Uncle Harry, if I say nothing to Gran about his crimes, she won't have to experience his betrayal and I'll have more money than I've ever dreamed of to spend on clothes and parties and everything else that makes my life go round . . . Or used to.

'Let's go back inside,' Mum says. 'I've left Leo with one of the nurses and I don't want to be away from him too long.'

'Of course,' says Gran, turning away.

Uncle Harry gives me a relieved nod. I can feel the crossroads melting away, a single path stretching out in front of me.

Grandad's motivational quote from yesterday flashes now in front of my mind's eye:

We are the choices we make.

'Wait, Gran,' I say. '*Wait*, there's something I need to tell you.'

THIRTY-SEVEN

Gran, turns back, eyebrows raised. She, Mum, Parvati and Uncle Harry all look at me.

'What is it, sweetheart?' Mum asks.

The sun beats down, warm on my face, as the 'nee-naw' of an ambulance sounds in the distance and I explain how I helped CJ break into the factory.

'Though you have to believe I didn't know what he was really planning,' I plead.

'Oh, Maya,' Mum says, her eyes brimming with tears.

'But *why*?' Gran shakes her head, appalled. 'I understand why some random eco fanatic might target us, but why would *you* want to hurt the company? You know we're as green as we can be.'

I gaze from face to face. Uncle Harry is watching me intently.

I take a deep breath.

'Uncle Harry's been stealing money from the company for most of the past year,' I say, trying to keep my voice steady.

Mum's hand flies to her mouth. Gran frowns. 'What?'

I explain about the faked receipts and illegal waste dumping. 'I . . . I know I should have come to you earlier, Gran,' I stammer, 'but . . . but I thought it was *you* who was trying to cut corners and save money.'

Gran grips the back of the bench. 'No . . .' She shakes her head. 'No, it's not true . . . it can't be . . .'

'Of course it's not true!' Uncle Harry cuts in sharply. 'I'd *never* hurt the company. I don't know why Maya would make all this up, but—'

'I'm not making anything up,' I insist.

'Maya wouldn't tell a lie like that,' Mum adds.

'Oh, wouldn't she?' Gran's face is stiff with fury. 'We just heard her admit that she's been lying since she arrived here.' She shoots Mum an angry look. 'Anyway, there's no way Harry would betray the company. It's in his *blood*.'

'It's in Maya's blood too.' A deep, hurt bitterness fills Mum's voice. 'Why do you assume it's Harry that's telling the truth?'

'I *am*,' insists Harry.

'You're not!' My voice rises. 'You're lying. You took Gran's money, and just now you offered me some of it to keep quiet.'

'How ridiculous,' Harry scoffs.

'It doesn't sound ridiculous to me,' Mum says.

It suddenly hits me why we haven't visited Gran and Grandad for so long: Gran has always taken Harry's side, believing him over Mum every time they argued. Making him special; making Mum feel like she was never good enough.

'Maya, this is completely unacceptable,' Gran says, her voice like ice. 'It's one thing being led astray by misguided friendships, but to accuse your own uncle . . .' She draws herself upright. 'I think perhaps it's time for your stay here to come to an end.'

Tears fill my eyes. Of all the possible outcomes, I hadn't considered this: that I'd explain everything to Gran and she wouldn't believe me.

'I'm telling the truth,' I say, my voice cracking.

Gran shakes her head. 'No, Maya,' she spits. 'You're lying and—'

'Maya's not lying.' Parvati sounds terrified, but determined.

Everyone turns to face her.

'I discovered the faked receipts a few days ago, while I was doing the deep dive into our waste protocols that you asked for, Ms Peyton,' Parvati explains, her eyes fixed on Gran. 'I should have come to you straight away, but – like Maya – I was worried you were behind the whole thing, so instead I went to Harry.' Her voice wobbles. 'He admitted what he'd done . . . and threatened to have me fired if I told you.'

'No.' Gran's face is ashen.

'This is ridiculous!' Harry explodes. 'Parvati's just upset because we dated a few times and I ended it. I'd never *threaten* her.'

'Of course you didn't.' Gran glares at Parvati. 'Everyone is just upset because of the fire. I suggest we all take a breath and calm down.'

She's refusing to accept the truth. I look from face to face, at the sneaky triumph creeping into Uncle Harry's eyes, at Mum shaking her head in frustration and at Parvati's trembling lips.

I take out my phone and open the recording app. *Please let this have worked.*

'Gran, please, just listen to this. It proves everything.'

'For goodness' sake,' Uncle Harry explodes.

'The first thing I thought about was undoing the changes I'd made to the company records . . .' His voice from a few minutes ago fills the air.

It's quickly followed, unmistakably, by mine: *'You mean deleting the evidence that you invented receipts and stole money?'*

Gran's eyes widen. Uncle Harry lunges for my phone, but Mum puts a hand on his arm to stop him. Gran leans towards the mobile as the recording continues. As she hears Uncle Harry talk about 'cutting a few corners', she gasps. A few moments later, when he attempts to bribe me, she groans, slumping onto the bench with her hands over her face.

'How dare you!' Mum growls, turning to Uncle Harry.

He stands, looking at us, his mouth gaping like he's trying to find something to say, searching for a way out. I switch off the recording. Gran looks up, despair etched on her face. Mum sits down beside her and holds her hand. For a moment, everyone is too shocked to speak. Uncle Harry bows his head.

'Gran?' My own voice is tiny.

She looks up at me, utterly defeated. 'Thank you, Maya,' she says, then her voice breaks: 'Oh, Harry.'

Uncle Harry gazes at her for a moment, then takes a swift step towards her. He briefly squeezes Gran's shoulder, then turns and, without looking at anyone else, walks away. Gran's mouth wobbles, tears now streaming down her cheeks. Parvati joins her and Mum on the bench. She slides her arm across Gran's back, stroking gently up and down.

I turn away and wander, shakily, back to the faded roses that Bear was staring at earlier. The edges of the pale pink petals are shrivelled and yellowing. As the sun beats down, I realize that never in my entire life have I felt as alone as I do right now.

I thought that I was doing something brave and daring when I set out to punish Gran for what I believed she had done. But, in fact, the really brave thing would have been to be honest with her. To confront her directly.

And I didn't. I was a coward.

That's the truth.

THIRTY-EIGHT

TWO WEEKS LATER

It's another really hot day. Ever since the factory fire the sun has been out and bright every morning, staying high in a clear blue sky for ages, then folding itself into a series of balmy, dusky evenings. There are more tourists than usual but, even so, the stretch of beach nearest Gran and Grandad's house is deserted.

Mum, Leo and I have got into the habit of coming here most afternoons. Mum has taken leave from work in order to be with us after the ordeal of the fire. Leo is actually coping really well, showing no signs of anxiety after his rooftop escape. We've just finished eating one of Grandad's picnic lunches, and Mum and Leo are paddling in the sea. I'm stretched out on a beach towel, thinking about the past few weeks. Not just the way my lies started and then spiralled out of control, but how close I came to losing my brother and my life. Bear's words echo in my head:

The only person you love is yourself.

A lot has happened during the past two weeks. After leaving us at the hospital, Uncle Harry went home, packed a bag, then vanished. He hasn't said where he is, though he's sent a couple messages to say that he's sorry and that he's okay.

For the first few days, Gran was in bits over his departure – and his betrayal. She stayed in her bedroom for hours on end, refusing to talk to anyone, even Grandad. On the fifth day she appeared at breakfast to announce that, although she wasn't going to press charges against Uncle Harry, she'd messaged him to say he no longer had his job at the factory and that she was planning on renting out his flat as a way of generating additional income for the rebuild.

Since then, she's dropped her appeal against the Harmony Earth Group, and has even had Drina and Val over to discuss ways of making Peyton Soaps super sustainable when it re-opens. I made a point of apologizing to them both when they came round, which they were really nice about.

I also asked about Bear, but it was obvious from the awkwardness of their reaction that he still doesn't want to see me.

At least Gran and Mum are getting on better. Mum's

even talking about us staying on in Cornwall after the summer. She's told her company she wants to relocate and is looking at houses and schools in Polborne. She's asked me several times if I'll mind – she's worried I'll miss my friends. But the truth is that I've got used to being without them – just as it's obvious they've got used to being without me.

Anyway, as one of Grandad's motivational quotes says:

What matters isn't where you live, but how you live.

And when I look back on my life in London, I realize how much of it revolved around going out in order to show off my new clothes and to get complimented on how I looked.

None of that seems to matter now. I don't think about things in the same way as I used to, and there's nothing I really want – other than for Bear to like me again.

Which, obviously, is never going to happen.

A fresh start is exactly what I need.

'Maya!' Mum's voice calls me back to the beach. 'Leo and I are heading inside. You coming?'

'In a bit,' I say, pushing myself up onto my elbows.

Mum waves, then calls to Leo. As they stroll off along the sand, I lean back on my towel again and close my eyes, letting the warm, salty breeze float across my arms and face.

'Hi, Maya,' says a familiar voice.

My eyes shoot open and I sit bolt upright. Bear is standing on the sand at my feet, a self-conscious half-smile on his face.

'Sorry,' he says, stepping back. 'I didn't mean to scare you.'

'No, no, you didn't.'

He's dressed in the same clothes as when I first met him: long shorts and a faded green T-shirt that reflects the colour of his eyes.

'How . . . how are you?' I stammer. 'How's your wrist?'

'It's fine,' Bear says. He folds his legs under him and sits on the end of my towel. The sun glints off his blond hair and I touch my own self-consciously.

We look at each other. My heart is hammering.

'Er, why are . . . what are you doing here?' I ask.

'I came to find you,' he says. 'I saw you with your mum and your brother. I waited until they left so . . .'

' . . . so you could talk to me?' I can hear the hope in my voice. Heat burns my cheeks.

Bear nods, awkwardly. 'I . . . I . . .' he hesitates. 'It was Skye . . . she kept nagging me to get in touch and see how you are.'

'Oh,' I say, 'that's nice of her.'

'But it was actually Rowan who made me walk over,' he says. 'She's fed up of me mooching around the camp feeling sorry for myself. That's what she said, anyway.'

'Sounds like Rowan.' I grin, but my heart is heavy. Bear's only here because his friend and his sister told him to come.

Bear smiles back. 'Yeah. Look, Ro overheard you at the hospital, when your uncle tried to bribe you? She told me that you'd told the truth to your family. About *everything*. Mum and Drina said something similar too. And that you apologized to them.'

'Oh,' I say, feeling bewildered. 'So . . . ?'

Bear hesitates. 'So I came to say that I'm sorry too . . . I was angry you'd lied to me, really angry, but . . . well, I guess you were only doing the best you could.'

A seagull squawks overhead, the waves swooshing along the shore.

I look up, into Bear's eyes. 'You were right to be angry.' Emotion swells in my chest. 'I lied, and one lie meant I had to tell another, and it all ended up spiralling out of control.' I pause, trying to control the shake in my voice.

'Anyway, I totally get why you wouldn't want to hang out with me ever again.'

'About that . . .' Bear's fingers reach across the beach towel, the tips just millimetres now from my own. 'You know, "ever again" is a very long time.' His forefinger rests lightly against mine. We look up, into each other's eyes. 'Maybe *too* long . . .' He grins.

We gaze at each other for a perfect moment. All the heartache that has been washing through me for weeks seeps away and a new emotion rises, up through my chest and my throat and onto my face, curving my lips into a smile.

Hope.

'I said I'd be home soon,' I say. 'Would you like to come too? You can meet my mum and my brother . . . and, afterwards, maybe we could hang out?'

Bear nods, his fingers twisting through mine, holding them tight. And then we get up, shake the sand off my towel and walk home, hand in hand, across the beach.

ACKNOWLEDGEMENTS

Truth or Dare wouldn't be here without the help of a huge number of people. Firstly – and crucially – my heartfelt thanks to Lucy Pearse, a phenomenal editor who always knows how to shape a story to make it the best possible version of itself. Also the entire design team at Simon & Schuster for an amazing cover; plus, Sophie Storr in production; Jane Pizzey and Katie Lawrence in editorial; copy-editor Sarah Hall and proofreader Leena Lane; Laura Hough, Leanne Nulty and Dani Wilson for their fantastic work in sales; and Dan Fricker and Eve Wersocki Morris for going above and beyond on marketing and publicity. I so appreciate your creativity and determination in making this book not just happen – but happen magnificently – and through the many challenges of a pandemic as well.

Thanks are also due to the team at United Agents, led by the incomparable Jodie Hodges, agent par excellence. I'm more grateful than I can say for everything you do to support me and my work.

I started writing *Truth or Dare* in the depths of lockdown

and I owe a massive debt of gratitude to the insightful writers with whom I shared drafts of my work and who took the time and trouble to give me their thoughts. They are credited on almost everything I produce and are always forensic in their observations and supportive - and no-nonsense – as they communicate them. Thank you for nineteen years of most excellent feedback: Lou Kuenzler, Moira Young, Melanie Edge, Julie Mackenzie and Gaby Halberstam.

Closer to home, I'd never have finished a book – let alone had one published – without my wonderful mum. Thank you, Mum, for always believing. Also my gratitude for their support to my dad, for reading everything I write (twice), to my brother for keeping my feet on the ground, to Dana for her endless empathy, and to Joe for being The Best and still sharing stories with me. And, finally, thank you to Eoin, who (especially on this book) has had no choice but to live and breathe my writing life on a daily basis. Thanks for being here, for making me laugh and for always knowing.

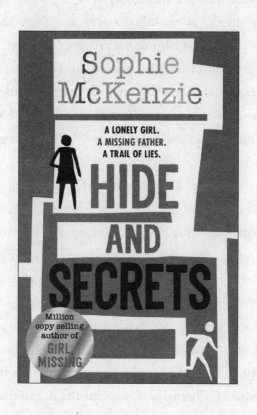

A LONELY GIRL.
A MISSING FATHER.
A TRAIL OF LIES.

HIDE AND SECRETS

Sophie McKenzie

Million copy selling author of *GIRL MISSING*

READ ON FOR A THRILLING EXTRACT FROM SOPHIE MCKENZIE'S HEARTSTOPPING THRILLER, *HIDE AND SECRETS*

1

Until the message arrived, there was no doubt in my mind: my dad was dead.

This wasn't the only thing I was certain about.

Back then, on that sunny morning in late July, I was also sure that the summer would end without me having a single friend, and that nothing exciting was ever going to happen to me while I lived in boring Brockledore.

As it turned out, on all those counts I was wrong . . .

Bess and I are sitting on a rug in the back garden, under the shade of the oak tree. I'm about to stroll over to the Barn. My head is already there, imagining the dress I've just pinned out, ready to cut. But Bess is just finishing a drawing, and I know she'll want to show it to me when she's done. Her tongue peeks out from between her lips as she concentrates on the last few strokes of her colouring pen. We don't look anything alike, Bess and I. She's got Dad's brown eyes and a heart-shaped face, framed by long, fine blond hair that's always escaping the bands Mum plaits it into.

I'm fairer-skinned with blue eyes. And my hair is short and spiky – like me.

'Cat! *Cat!*' Mum is calling from the house. I can just see her pink rope sandals out of the corner of my eye. I don't look up. Everything about her is Just. So. Irritating.

'What does she want now?' I mutter.

'*Cat!*' The pink sandals stomp across the grass.

Bess stiffens. She hates it when Mum and I get mad with each other.

'Why didn't you answer?' Mum demands, arriving at the edge of the rug. She waves her arms in the air so violently that her bangles collide in a clash of tinkles. 'I was calling for ages.'

'Sorry,' I say, trying to keep the fact that I'm not at all sorry out of my voice. 'I was *miles* away.' I'm deliberately using one of Mum's favourite phrases. She tends to flutter her hands when she uses it, presumably to indicate how easily distracted she gets by alternate spiritual planes.

Mum glares at me, clearly picking up on my sarcastic undertones. She has clients today, so she's wearing one of her waftier outfits: a crimson sundress with rainbow chiffon frills under a fringed pink shawl that's pinned to the straps of her dress with several of her astrological sign brooches.

2

Mum's a celebrity astrologer who used to be famous. Not movie-star-level famous, but well-known enough that people would stare when she took me to primary school. I *loved* that when I was little. Back then she had a weekly slot on a morning TV show to run through 'what the stars have in store this weekend'. She denies it if anyone asks, but I reckon she'd give anything to be back there on the nation's screens every week. She certainly laps it up when anyone recognizes her now.

'There's something I need you to do this morning, Cat,' she says, brushing a stray red curl off her face. I know for a fact Mum's hair is really as straight and dark as my own, but she seems to think her clients prefer wild red curls washed through with hot-pink streaks.

'What?' I gaze up at her warily.

'Darling, don't look at me like that.' She sighs. 'You need to clear all your . . . your *scraps* out of the barn this morning.'

My jaw drops. '*What?*'

'And once you've done that, a quick dust and vacuum. Right now, Cat, please?'

'But that's so unfair!' I blurt out, my voice rising to a shout.

I can't believe it. The Barn is a cottage on the other side of our back garden. Mum has plans to use it next year as a guest house for her wealthy clients, but right now it's empty. The attic room there, with its wall of glass windows, is the perfect place for me to spread out my designs and store all the fabrics I've accumulated since I started dress-making earlier this year.

'Why do I have to clear my stuff out?' I protest. Beside me, Bess tenses with anxiety. I try to swallow down my temper. 'I've pinned a dress with a skirt I'm going to cut on the bias. It's all laid out like I want it.'

Mum frowns. 'Mrs Trimble's already picked your bits and pieces off the floor. They're in boxes by the Barn front door.'

'What?' I leap to my feet, my fury surging uncontrollably. 'But I'm in the middle of making my dress. Why did she do that?'

'Because I asked her to,' Mum snaps. 'But it left her short on time, which is why you need to run the vacuum cleaner round to make the place—'

'No! *Please*, Mum, I *need* the Barn. I'm *using* it.'

Mum glares at me. 'Well, you can't use it any more,' she snaps. 'Now hurry up – the Tuesdays will be here in a couple of hours.'

What is she talking about?

'Who are the Tuesdays?' I demand.

Mum rolls her eyes. 'The mosaic specialist who's going

4

to renovate the courtyard, and his son. They'll be staying in the Barn for a few weeks. I'm sure I told you about them the other day, Cat.'

My jaw drops. This is typical Mum, ruining my life in order to spend money on stuff we don't need. It's ironic: she's always making out how spiritual she is, but the truth is she's been super-materialistic ever since Dad died.

Bess tugs at the hem of my shorts. I glance down at her. She stamps her foot; it's her signal that I should stop arguing.

I ignore it.

'So you're saying that not only do I have to give up all my plans to make dresses in the Barn, but a random man and his random son are moving into it? For the whole summer?'

'Stop making such a ridiculous fuss.' Mum's bangles clink loudly again as she points in the direction of the barn. 'Fetch your boxes so the poor Tuesdays don't trip over them, then dust and vacuum. *Now.*'

She stomps off, leaving me open-mouthed. Bess tugs at my shorts again. I glance down. She makes a goofy face, sticking out her tongue and crossing her eyes. She can see I'm upset and is trying to make me laugh.

Something twists in my stomach. 'I'm fine,' I say.

Bess raises her eyebrows as if to ask: *really?*

I nod. 'Really.'

She goes back to her drawing: a puppy with dark splotches on its white fur and a dark brown patch over one eye. Bess has been obsessed with puppies ever since our dog, Pirate, was run over the week before Dad died. Because she's mean, Mum refuses to let us have another pet, so Bess draws one new 'Pirate' after another. Her pictures are amazing. Way better than you'd expect from an average almost-seven-year-old. We both get our creative talent from Dad. He worked in a fancy jewellery shop, but he always said he was really a frustrated designer.

He died on his boat, in a storm out at sea almost eighteen months ago. I still miss him every day: the way he let me put golden syrup on my toast when Mum wasn't looking; how he took me and Bess out sailing every weekend, always happy, even when it poured with rain. And his huge goodnight hugs that smelled of soap and sawdust, that made me feel like I was totally safe and that nothing bad could ever happen.

'I'd better go to the Barn.' I force a smile for Bess's sake. Before we lost Dad, she used to irritate me. I was mean to her, always telling her off for following me around or teasing her for playing with stupid dolls even though she was only little. She used to say stuff like, 'please let me play, Cat, please'. And I'd always run off too fast for her to follow, her wails echoing in my ears.

I hate how I acted then.

She's almost seven now, and I'd give anything to have her ask me to let her play.

But she doesn't ask. In fact, she doesn't say anything at all.

Bess hasn't said a word – to anyone – since Dad died. For the first few months, Mum kept saying we just needed to give her time. But it's been well over a year now and Bess has got into the habit of not saying anything at all.

Worse, we've all got into the habit of not expecting her to.

The cardboard boxes full of my sewing stuff are just inside the front door of the Barn. The fabric for the dress I've been pinning is in a jumbled heap in the top box, the pattern fluttering loose and to the side. Pinning anything cut on the bias is really tricky. It took me ages to get the pattern in exactly the right place and now I'll have to start all over again.

The vacuum cleaner stands expectantly next to the stack of boxes. I glare at it. This is so unfair. There's nowhere in the house with enough space and light for me to do my dressmaking and Mum knows it. My bedroom is small and gloomy. I've been wanting to move into the spare room for ages – it's huge with lots of space and big windows that let in loads of natural light, perfect for dressmaking. But Mum keeps it cluttered to bursting point with crystals and astrological ornaments and all the old designer outfits she doesn't have room for in her wardrobe.

I pick up the boxes, anger still hot in my chest. No way am I doing the stupid dusting and vacuum-cleaning. I stomp off, across the courtyard then around the side of our house. I dump the boxes in the front porch. I'll pick them up later; right now I have to get away from Mum. From all of it.

I hurry along the drive and into the woods. I pick my way along the winding path down through the trees to the road, then stroll the fifty yards or so into the village. Brockledore is tiny: there's a pub, a grocery store with a post office, a cafe that sells chips and sandwiches and an antique showroom, as well as a handful of pottery shops and boutiques selling old-fashioned clothes.

I stand at the war memorial, opposite the bus stop and gaze along the familiar high street, resentment burning inside me. I used to walk down here with Dad sometimes. He'd always give me some cash to spend on sweets in the grocery store and everyone we passed on the way would say 'hello'. Dad would never have let Mum take the Barn attic away from me. He'd understand why I needed it. Yes, if he was still here, he wouldn't let Mum be so greedy, basing all her decisions on how much money she can either spend or make. He'd let Bess have another dog and he *definitely* wouldn't allow a couple of strangers to live in the Barn over the summer to make a stupid mosaic in the stupid courtyard.

But Dad is gone.

And Mum is determined to make my life miserable.

Learning to pin and sew designs is basically all I've wanted to do for the past six months. Mum just doesn't understand. I've found something for myself that's a million miles away from the way she uses astrology to manipulate money out of people. Dressmaking is creative, like Dad was – I can lose myself in it. Now I don't know what I'm going to do for the rest of the summer holidays. It's not like I've got any friends I can hang out with.

Feeling sulky and cross, I wander back through the woods that lead home. The sun is shining and the birds are singing, but with every step I feel more depressed. I emerge from the trees onto the lane that leads up to our house. My phone rings and I glance down. I don't recognize the number.

I've been told a million times to be wary of random callers. But that isn't why I reject this call – I just don't feel like talking to anyone. The sun beats down on my head, the only sound the crunch of the gravel under my feet and the soft sway of the trees in the breeze. My phone rings again.

Man, they're persistent.

I close the call again and am just about to block the number, when my phone pings with a text. I gaze down. It's the same caller.

Hello, Cat. I'm Rik. A friend of your dad's. I'd like to talk to you.

My stomach contracts with shock. A creeping anxiety twists through me. Dad's been dead for a year and a half. How would a friend of his have my number? And why would they be calling me and not Mum?

This feels wrong. Another message:

Please call me, Cat. I need to tell you something. It's important.

Why doesn't he text whatever it is? Whoever this Rik is, he's doing all the wrong things to get me to speak to him.

Irritated, I text back:

What's so important?

I wait for a second, my finger hovering over the block icon. And then a third message comes through. An answer to my question that makes so little sense it feels like my brain is crashing.

Your dad is alive.

Sophie McKenzie

Discover the bestselling MISSING SERIES from the queen of teen thrillers.

A 2022 World Book Day Book

SIMON &
SCHUSTER

ABOUT THE AUTHOR

Sophie McKenzie is the multi award-winning original queen of teen thrillers, whose 2005 debut, *Girl, Missing*, remains a YA bestseller. She has followed its success with two further books in the Missing series: *Sister, Missing* and *Missing Me*, as well as the World Book 2022 title *Boy, Missing* and many other teen thriller and romance novels, including The Medusa Project series, *Hide and Secrets* and *Truth or Dare*. Sophie's first adult novel, *Close My Eyes*, was selected for the Richard and Judy Book Club. Sophie's books have sold more than a million copies in the UK alone and are translated and sold all over the world. She lives in North London.

www.sophiemckenziebooks.com
Instagram @sophiemckenziebooks
Twitter @sophiemckenzie_